Razi felt a sur... triumph—not t... outcome had ever been in any doubt.

Lucy had needs and he had urges. It was a match that would last for precisely one night. He'd leave her happy, but he'd leave. His playboy life was over. Duty beckoned, and he was ready to serve.

He smiled as she came shyly toward him, all buttoned up and ready to be undressed. He'd serve Lucy Tennant, and then he'd serve Isla de Sinnebar with the same focus and energy—though for a lifetime rather than a single night.

SUSAN STEPHENS was a professional singer before meeting her husband on the tiny Mediterranean island of Malta. In true Harlequin Presents style they met on Monday, became engaged on Friday and were married three months later. Almost thirty years and three children later they are still in love. (Susan does not advise her children to return home one day with a similar story as she may not take the news with the same fortitude as her own mother!)

Susan had written several nonfiction books when fate took a hand. At a charity costume ball there was an after-dinner auction. One of the lots, "Spend a Day with an Author," had been donated by Harlequin Presents® author Penny Jordan. Susan's husband bought this lot and Penny was to become not just a great friend, but a wonderful mentor who encouraged Susan to write romance.

Susan loves her family, her pets, her friends and her writing. She enjoys entertaining, travel and going to the theater. She reads, cooks and plays the piano to relax, and can occasionally be found throwing herself off mountains on a pair of skis or galloping through the countryside.

Visit Susan's Web site, www.susanstephens.net.
She loves to hear from her readers
all around the world!

RULING SHEIKH, UNRULY MISTRESS
SUSAN STEPHENS

~ P.S. I'm Pregnant! ~

HARLEQUIN®

TORONTO • NEW YORK • LONDON
AMSTERDAM • PARIS • SYDNEY • HAMBURG
STOCKHOLM • ATHENS • TOKYO • MILAN • MADRID
PRAGUE • WARSAW • BUDAPEST • AUCKLAND

If you purchased this book without a cover you should be aware that this book is stolen property. It was reported as "unsold and destroyed" to the publisher, and neither the author nor the publisher has received any payment for this "stripped book."

Recycling programs
for this product may
not exist in your area.

ISBN-13: 978-0-373-52775-5

RULING SHEIKH, UNRULY MISTRESS

First North American Publication 2010.

Copyright © 2010 by Susan Stephens.

All rights reserved. Except for use in any review, the reproduction or utilization of this work in whole or in part in any form by any electronic, mechanical or other means, now known or hereafter invented, including xerography, photocopying and recording, or in any information storage or retrieval system, is forbidden without the written permission of the publisher, Harlequin Enterprises Limited, 225 Duncan Mill Road, Don Mills, Ontario, Canada M3B 3K9.

This is a work of fiction. Names, characters, places and incidents are either the product of the author's imagination or are used fictitiously, and any resemblance to actual persons, living or dead, business establishments, events or locales is entirely coincidental.

This edition published by arrangement with Harlequin Books S.A.

For questions and comments about the quality of this book please contact us at Customer_eCare@Harlequin.ca.

® and TM are trademarks of the publisher. Trademarks indicated with ® are registered in the United States Patent and Trademark Office, the Canadian Trade Marks Office and in other countries.

www.eHarlequin.com

Printed in U.S.A.

RULING SHEIKH, UNRULY MISTRESS

PROLOGUE

'DARKER than night and twice as dangerous' was how the magazine he'd snaffled from his secretary's desk referred to the al Maktabi brothers. Razi al Maktabi replaced it with a wink at the only woman who knew how he took his coffee.

Razi's lips were still curving when he shut his office door. The media was struggling for dirt on him, apparently. Coming to a halt in front of a wall of windows, he placed his first call. While he waited for it to connect he studied a gunmetal slice of the Thames, where the never-ending action soothed him. Across the river, in what felt like touching distance from his penthouse, stood the Houses of Parliament, while behind him was the sleek cocoon of the CEO of Maktabi Communications, a company he had driven to international prominence. Ahead of him lay the Phoenix throne of the Isla de Sinnebar, but before he assumed the duties of his desert kingdom he was calling one last reunion.

The magazine article had got some things right, Razi reflected as the telephone droned in Lord Thomas Spencer-Dayly's Gloucestershire mansion. Razi's elder brother, Sheikh Ra'id al Maktabi, was every bit as hard as the journalist supposed and with good reason. Their father had sown enough wild oats to seed the whole of the American Midwest and there were numerous pretenders to Ra'id's Sapphire throne.

This went some way to explaining why Ra'id ruled mainland Sinnebar with a rod of iron, earning him the sobriquet 'The Sword of Vengeance' by those who liked a lick of Hollywood with their sheikh. The journalist had left one thing out. Razi would die for the brother who had made his childhood bearable, and who had fought for him to share the same rights Ra'id enjoyed as their father's legitimate son...

Razi's face lit as the voice of his closest friend came on the line.

'What's up, bad boy?' Tom growled, sounding as if he had just climbed out of bed.

Razi outlined his proposal.

'The press turning up the heat?' Tom suggested with amusement.

'They don't bother me. I'm more interested in us taking one last break before I assume control.'

The air between London and Gloucestershire stilled. Both men knew the seriousness of the task awaiting Razi. The moment he was hailed ruling Sheikh of the Isla de Sinnebar, Razi would immerse himself in caring for his people. 'It's a task I relish, Tom.'

'I know...I know.'

Tom had his serious side too, but today was all about lifting his best friend's mood. 'I can't pick up a newspaper without seeing your ugly face staring back at me,' he complained. 'I've got the morning press right here.'

Razi's lips tugged with amusement. Brought to Tom's suite of rooms having been ironed first by his butler, no doubt.

'Here's just one example…'

Furious rustling ensued as Tom attempted to tame the broadsheets. 'Can the playboy prince work the same magic on the Isla de Sinnebar as he has on Maktabi Communications.'

'I've heard it, Tom,' Razi interrupted good-naturedly.

'They say you're a danger to women everywhere.'

'Business is my passion,' Razi cut across Tom flatly. And now he would turn those skills to the management of a country.

'And the women?' Tom pressed, not ready yet to let him off the hook.

'I have a vacancy.' And could be as dangerous as any woman wanted him to be.

Tom laughed. 'That shouldn't take long to fill. This journalist describes you and Ra'id as educated muscle.'

'Yes, I rather liked that,' Razi admitted, succumbing to Tom's good mood with a grin. 'Doesn't it go on to say we've proved ourselves to be fighters and lovers of unparalleled vigour?'

'Was the woman talking from personal experience?'

'Hang on while I rack my brain for memorable encounters with someone audacious enough to take notes while I made love to her.'

Tom laughed and read on. 'It's Razi al Maktabi's unforgiving gaze and striking physique, clothed in misleadingly sedate Savile Row, that gives him the edge, in the opinion of this writer.'

Razi's looks were the result of a union between the Middle East and middle England, but even he would admit they were unusual. Emerald eyes contrasted sharply with the jet-black hair and deep bronze complexion of his

Bedouin ancestors, and it was said he had the eyes and lips of the courtesan who had bewitched his father.

The same courtesan who had dumped him in the arms of whichever child-care professional court officials had seen fit to appoint. But that was another story. He'd moved on. He wasn't interested in looking back, breaking hearts or taking revenge. On the contrary, he adored women. His love for them had remained undiminished throughout numerous attempts to trap him into marriage. As had his determination never to be tied down.

'Enough,' Razi exclaimed as Tom started reading another article about him. 'Are you coming skiing with me or not?'

As he might have predicted Tom embraced his suggestion with enthusiasm. The ski company was a small part of Razi's business empire and he kept it for pleasure rather than gain, moving to a different chalet each year, both to test them for his guests and to keep the press guessing. Was there any better way of celebrating life, loyalty and friendship before the duties and responsibilities of ruling a country ruled him than this one last trip into the mountains?

Tom gave a short, masculine laugh. 'Though we'll have to put a bag over your head if we're to get any peace from the ladies.'

'With you and the rest of the boys around I'll blend into the crowd.'

'Really?' Tom murmured dryly.

'This is a boys-only trip. There won't be a woman in sight.'

'With you involved I find that hard to believe,' Tom argued in the upper-class drawl that always made Razi smile. 'How do you intend keeping them away?'

'That's your job, Tom.' He was lapping up this return to

the easy humour they'd shared as boys at school and then later in the special forces. 'You always were my first choice of wing man. Just watch my back.'

'And if it's a frontal attack?'

Razi's lips settled in a smile of happy anticipation at the thought of all the beautiful women in the world waiting to be adored. 'In that case, Tom, wait for my signal.'

CHAPTER ONE

S<small>HE</small> had the list of this week's guests clutched so tightly in her hand her knuckles had turned white.

'Hey, Luce, what's the problem?' demanded Fiona, another member of the elite chalet staff as she snuck out of the chalet Fiona's usual good half-hour early. 'You look like you got some troublesome guests coming to stay.'

'No particular problem,' Lucy Tennant replied distractedly over Fiona's hearty laugh, glancing deep into the flames of the aromatic pine log fire Lucy had lit earlier. Was it only minutes before she had been feeling on top of the world? Shouldn't she still be feeling elated? She had just opened a letter explaining she had been voted top chalet girl both by her colleagues and by her employers and it was the first time she'd won anything, let alone an acknowledgement that meant so much to her. But along with that letter had come this list itemising the preferences of that week's guests, and for some reason, having read it, her confidence had shrunk to the size of a pea.

Tom Spencer-Dayly: no special requests.

Sheridan Dalgleath: Porridge made with salt, plenty

of single malt to drink and any beef served must be Aberdeen Angus.

William Montefiori: Only fresh pasta, never dried, please.

Theo Constantine: Good champagne—lots of it.

One other:

It was the world of white that yawned after the fateful words *One other* that had got to her. For some reason it had sent a shiver down her spine. There was also an addendum to let Lucy know that two bodyguards would be travelling with the party, one of whom, Omar Farouk, would be housed on the top floor, while the second, Abu Bakr, would take the small bedroom opposite the ski room.

The clients must be people with serious connections, Lucy reasoned, hence the unusual level of security and her apprehension. She had to remind herself that she'd seen it all before. Each week head office sent her the same standard form detailing the needs and expectations of the new arrivals and she always felt a little anxious, wanting not just to meet expectations, but to exceed them.

But she had never felt as uneasy as this before, Lucy realised, checking each line again. The list was quite straightforward. Which should have been enough to stop the shivers running up and down her spine, but wasn't.

To calm her nerves she reasoned things through. This was one of the most expensive rental chalets in one of the most expensive ski resorts in the world. She was hardly a stranger to wealthy people, their needs, or the entourages that travelled with them. In fact, compared to most, this group appeared small and quite reasonable in their demands. Experience suggested a group of men would be mad keen to be on the slopes every daylight hour so she'd hardly see them, other than at mealtimes. Their main requirement would be lots of good food, plenty of hot water and clean towels and a never-ending supply of liquid refreshment when they got back to the chalet. With brothers of her own, it wasn't long before she was starting to feel a lot more confident.

They would almost certainly be public-school edu-cated, Lucy mused, studying the names again. So one man preferred to remain anonymous—there could be any number of reasons why that should be and none of them her business.

Stroking back a wisp of honey-coloured hair, she real-ised it was the note scrawled in ink on the bottom of the page that set alarm bells ringing: 'If anyone can cope with this group, Lucy, we know, you can—' Translated loosely, that said she was less likely to make a fuss if the clients were more demanding and difficult than usual, because Lucy Tennant was not only a highly qualified cordon bleu chef, but a quiet girl, a good girl, a girl who took pride in her job managing the company's most prestigious chalet, someone who worked diligently without complaint. Her line manager knew this. So why did she get the feeling there was something he wasn't telling her?

She shook herself round. Time was moving on. With Fiona's social life making heavy demands on Fiona's working hours, there was always plenty of work at the chalet for Lucy. But the crystal-clear alpine light was streaming in, tempting her outside…

Pushing back the quaint, carved chair, she went to draw the cherry-red gingham curtains a little way across the ecru lace to stare out wistfully. It seemed such a shame to close out the perfect mountain day, but if she didn't she'd never get to work.

Work had always been enough for her—and working here, where she could almost taste the freedom of the mountains, the silence, the space, the intoxicating air.

And the loneliness…

Working here was fantastic, Lucy thought fiercely, blotting out the rest. A pang of loneliness was inevitable in a chic French town where everyone seemed to be part of a couple. She'd always known she would be on the outside looking in. It was a small price to pay to be part of so much energy and fun. Shy, plump and plain was never going to be a recipe for non-stop action in a community where glamorous, confident people revelled in using their bodies to the full—and not just for skiing. But she could cook for them and she could make a chalet cosy and welcoming, which had always been reward enough.

And one day my prince will come, Lucy mused wryly, fingering the tiny silver shoe she wore for luck around her neck—though whether he'd notice her amongst so many beautiful, sleek, toned bodies seemed highly unlikely.

'See ya—'

The front door slammed and moments later she saw Fiona throwing her arms around the neck of her latest conquest.

Lucy pulled back from the window, knowing the snow scene and towering mountains with spears of brilliant light shooting through their jagged granite peaks were just a magical starting point. What she really valued was the good-natured camaraderie of her colleagues and the guests who gave her real purpose in life. Everything she lacked at home in the bosom of a relentlessly book-bound family living in the centre of a smoky, noisy city was here in this part-tamed wilderness of unimaginable icy splendour.

She loved books too, Lucy reflected, dipping down to look inside the fridge, but she liked to put what she read into practice, to experience things in reality. That was why she was here in a picturesque corner of an alpine village with a stream gurgling happily outside the pitched-roof wooden chalet, feeling reassured by the sight of the delicious local cheeses, along with the milk and cream she had sourced from the neighbouring farms. She still found it hard to believe that little Lucy, as her brothers still insisted on calling her, could negotiate the best of terms with local artisan producers, or that she held such a position of responsibility as a chalet chef for the ski season with the top company in Val d'Isere.

But she had paid her dues, Lucy remembered wryly, logging the items she would need to order for the week ahead before closing the door. She had come to France from a top restaurant in England where she had worked her way up from the bottom to the point where she received praise, as well as that all important reference, or *lettre de recommendation*, from Monsieur Roulet himself. Catering for demanding clients would never be easy, but she loved the challenge of the work as well as the opportunity it had given her to break free from her brothers' shadow.

Lucy's six brothers all excelled in areas her mother and father valued far more than cooking and it saddened Lucy to know she had never found a way to please her parents. Her self-respect had taken a real hit on the day her mother had alarmingly confided that they didn't know what to do with a girl—especially one who cooked. Her mother had said this as if a passion for cooking were somehow degrading for a woman, and when she had added in her airy, distracted way that it was better for Lucy to stay close to home and cook for her family where there was no chance of getting herself into trouble, Lucy had known it was time to leave.

Get herself into trouble? Some hope!

Lucy's wry smile returned. Her mother would no doubt applaud the irony that led men to treat Lucy as though she were their kid sister. At least she had escaped from other people's expectations of her, and thanks to her own endeavours, had the chance to discover who she was. She knew she wanted to make a difference in life and if that meant giving people pleasure with her cooking then she asked for nothing more.

Her breakout moment from home had been the first time in her life she'd done anything unexpected. She had been prepared to wash dishes for however long it took until she could persuade Monsieur Roulet to take her on, and had been amazed when the ferocious chef had granted her one of his sought-after training places, and even more surprised when her training had finished and he'd said she should see something of the world and that he would personally recommend her. Not wanting to disappoint the man who had launched her career, she had come up with an audacious plan to cater a dinner party for the director of one the world's most celebrated chalet companies. It was such a novel approach the woman had accepted and the rest was history. Lucy had returned home that night in triumph, and had sat patiently through the usual heated academic discussion taking place around a dinner table littered with dirty plates. Each time a break had come in the conversation she had tried to explain her exciting news, but her mother had hushed her and turned back to the boys, so Lucy's opportunity to share her happiness had never come. She still wasn't sure anyone had noticed her heaving her suitcase out of the house.

Enough reminiscing! She'd lose the job she loved if she didn't get moving! Fiona leaving early meant there were still beds to be made and floors to be swept and washed, but at least the food was ready. In fact, if it weren't for Mr One Other making her heart judder with apprehension she'd have a happy day ahead of her, doing all the things she liked best.

Razi scrunched the letter in his fist. It had been couriered to the helicopter taking him from Geneva to Val d'Isere and made him want to grab the old guard in Isla de Sinnebar by the collective throat and tell them, No way!

But that would mean cancelling this trip.

He barely noticed the sensational landscape of ice-capped peaks. Promised in marriage to a cousin he had never met? He realised his throne was the real prize—and not just the throne of Isla de Sinnebar. From his kingdom it was a short stride across the channel to the mainland and Ra'id's throne. But if anyone thought they could turn him against his brother—

His anger turned to cold fury as he ripped open the package that accompanied the letter. In his hand was a photograph. He studied the image of a beautiful young girl. She was his distant cousin Leila, apparently. Leila's long black hair was lush, but her eyes were sad. She was as beautiful as any girl he'd ever seen, but he felt nothing for her. It was like looking at a beautiful painting and registering the perfection of its composition without wanting to hang it on his wall.

'Poor Leila,' he murmured, feeling some sympathy for

a girl who clearly understood she was being used as a bargaining counter by her unscrupulous relatives.

Wrapping up the picture in its silken cover, he stuffed it into the net at the side of his seat. He would not be trapped into marriage by parent, child, or a council of elders. When he married, it would be to a girl of his choice; a girl so cool, so keenly intelligent and effortlessly sophisticated, she would make a Hollywood movie star look clumsy.

Disaster! She'd spilled everything! Canapés littered the floor. The floor was awash with champagne. One man was mopping his jeans, while Mr One Other stared at her, frowning.

Even her training under the strictest of chefs could never have prepared her for her first encounter with the mysterious One Other. Tall, bronzed and serious about working out, he was a formidable force in the room and in the space of a condemning glance had reduced her to a dithering wreck.

Everything ruined in the blink of an eye. She would be sacked for this. Lucy's eyes welled with tears at the thought. She had planned so carefully, getting up at four to prepare the chalet and start cooking for the new guests.

She had left nothing to chance. There was a log fire blazing in the hearth, and fresh flowers she had arranged herself to bring the delicate fragrance of the French countryside into a chalet so clean you could eat the cordon bleu feast she had created off the lovingly polished oak floors. The menu she had devised encompassed every delicacy she could think of to tempt the palates of sophisticated men. Those men were currently lounging on the sofa, their faces registering varying degrees of surprise at her ineptitude, while the man in the shadows, the man who had compelled her attention from the moment she left the kitchen, gave off an impression of biting reproof. Her lovingly prepared tray of canapés was upturned in a puddle of vintage champagne and she had not only knocked the tray off the table when her gaze had locked with his, but had sprayed the designer jeans of a man whom, apart from the striking good looks he shared with his companions, she had barely noticed at all. Her attention had been wholly focused on the stranger staring at her now, and in holding that stare she had caught the toe of her shoe beneath the rug and had blundered forward.

How could a man standing in shade give off so much light? How could green eyes burn so fiercely? How could a man framed by four astonishingly good-looking friends eclipse them completely?

Breaking eye contact with him, she determinedly shook herself back to the task in hand. She had worked hard for this job and had no intention of losing it in the space of one compelling stare. 'My apologies, gentlemen—if you will allow me to, I will quickly repair the damage—'

Then *He* stepped forward, blotting out the light. 'Don't you think we should complete the introductions first?'

There was no warmth in his voice. That was not a suggestion, but an order, she concluded, quickly trying to collect the crushed canapés from the floor. 'Yes, sorry—' She looked up, only to find her gaze level with a part of him that shocked her rigid. Jerking her head up past the heavy belt securing his jeans, and on over the tactile dark blue top he wore with the sleeves pushed back revealing muscular arms, she saw a face of impossible design, a face so strong and beautiful she could have stared at it for ever. He had wild, thick, blue-black hair that caressed his chiselled cheekbones and fell in heavy waves across his proud, smooth brow, while some of it had caught on sideburns that mingled with the night-dark stubble on his face.

Wow, she thought silently, standing up.

Wow again. *One Other* was a mountain of a man, a man with hard green eyes and an uncompromising mouth. She didn't need to be told that he was the lead guest, and not just the lead guest, but the leader of the pack. The man with the voice like bitter chocolate was the man she had to please or lose her job. No wonder he came with a not so subtle warning, she thought, remembering the scrawled note from her manager on that week's guest list.

She was still standing speechless when the kind man called Tom came to her assistance. 'And this is Lucy,' he announced smoothly.

Having introduced her, Tom stepped back.

CHAPTER TWO

R<small>AZI</small> took in the trail of collapsed canapés on the floor, and yet more crushed in the girl's hands. Being ever the gentleman, Tom was being careful to hide his thoughts, but it was clear to him that the blushing, flustered girl currently hopping from foot to foot in front of him wasn't up to the job. She had gone to pieces like her canapés, spilling expensive champagne all over the floor as well as over William Montefiori's jeans.

'It's nothing,' William murmured, with relaxed charm, easing away from the promise of more disaster. 'I'll go and change.'

Razi was not so forgiving. His thumb was already caressing the speed dial to his personal chef.

'Allow me,' his friend Theo cut in with a predictably wolfish smile. Removing the cloth from the girl's hands, Theo proceeded to hold her troubled stare as he dabbed ineffectually at the puddle of champagne.

'For goodness' sake—' Razi's whiplash tone prompted Tom to snatch the cloth from Theo and repair the damage as quickly as he could. Razi doubted either of them had ever held a cleaning cloth in their life and wouldn't be doing so now if they hadn't some intention of getting into the girl's knickers. As for the girl, she was too badly shaken up to do anything—shaken up by what, exactly, he'd find out later.

'Lucy,' Tom repeated discreetly in his ear. 'Lucy Tennant, our chef and chalet girl.'

'Lucy…' His friends faded into the background. The girl was visibly trembling. He saw how young she was then and flashed a reprimanding glance at Theo. The girl was not only unused to such an imbalance of female hormones and testosterone she was terrified of losing her job.

'Pleased to meet you, sir.'

In her favour, her voice was musical, her stare direct, but that was no excuse for ineptitude. He employed the best across his organisation; only the best.

'Lucy won the chalet girl of the year award,' Tom broke in helpfully.

'Thank you, Tom,' he murmured in a voice that clearly said, Not now. Tom's soft heart was one thing, but he was conscious of how slender a thread his leisure time hung on and how soon this last ski-break indulgence would end. When he looked at the girl he was working out how much incompetence he was prepared to put up with before he ordered in his own staff and they took over.

'And you are?' she asked tentatively, her cheeks pinking up as she made a last stab at maintaining the formalities.

He looked at Tom for inspiration.

'Mac?' Tom suggested with a shrug.

'Mac,' the girl repeated shyly.

Their gazes remained locked and her grip was warm and firm as they shook hands, though she removed her hand from his faster than he would have liked. The report he'd received about her said she was self-possessed, calm, intelligent, organised, multilingual and a cordon bleu chef. The last two he had no proof of yet—strike the rest.

Then she surprised him.

'Once again, I apologise,' she said, almost literally shaking herself round. 'I hope the accident won't spoil your enjoyment of the meal I have prepared.'

'Not at all,' Tom chipped in, falling silent when Razi shot him a warning stare.

But something did smell good. 'What's on the menu?' he demanded.

She brightened and immediately proved to be one of those people who could deliver a menu and make the palate sing with greedy anticipation.

'Freshly made French onion soup topped with a slice of Parmesan baguette, followed by crispy duck breast in a fruit reduction, with a chocolate torte and cinder-toffee ice cream to follow.'

'I say,' Tom exclaimed, while his other friends sighed happily, prepared to forgive her anything now. Even Razi was inclined to give her the benefit of the doubt. If Lucy could deliver what she'd promised she could stay with his blessing too.

'Tom,' he said, still staring deep into Lucy's complex turquoise gaze, 'would you kindly ring the chalet company?' In spite of Lucy's calm, sweet voice, tumultuous thoughts were still boiling behind her eyes. With his last words that tumult had turned to panic. She was certain he would not give her another chance, and she looked utterly devastated. It was then he came to a decision that surprised even him. 'Would you tell them we don't need any more staff hanging round? But we'd like Lucy to stay—Abu and Omar can handle anything else we require.'

She slumped with relief, but then another thought must have occurred to her because the panic was back.

'You'll be quite safe with us,' he promised dryly as she took a jerky step away from him. 'We're here to ski.' His lips tugged. 'You'll hardly see us.'

She swallowed deep. 'That's what I thought,' she said awkwardly, her cheeks blooming a deeper shade of scarlet.

You may go, he might have said at this point, had they been in the old palace on the Isla de Sinnebar, but this was both a different and more complex situation. Lucy worked for him and yet this situation demanded more of them both. The intimacy of a chalet was very different from life in a palace. She'd put her own stamp on the chalet, he noticed—personal touches. There were fresh flowers on the table, and fruit that looked as if it had been picked that morning. Cakes and biscuits, still warm from the oven, tempted with their delicious aroma, and there were books and a couple of decks of cards. He liked being spoiled—what man didn't? She had done every-thing she could think of to make them welcome. Cer-tainly, she could stay.

Seeing she was still uncomfortable after her bad start, he asked her discreetly, 'Would you like me to call Omar and Abu to help you?'

'Oh, no,' she exclaimed, her eyes widening with a genuine desire to please that turned up the heat from hot to scorching. While he was admiring pearl-white teeth he could so easily imagine nipping him in passion she was glancing across the large, open-plan sitting room to her much smaller kitchen area. 'I don't mean to be difficult,' she explained, 'but my cooking space is very small—'

'And you prefer to do things your way?' he suggested,

inhaling her wildflower scent. It was a surprise to be so attracted to such subtle charm, but then novelty was the most valuable currency of all to men who had everything.

'I love my work, and I'm not very good at having people interfere.'

'Really?' A smile creased his face. 'Than I shall be sure to keep everyone away from you.'

'You're teasing me,' she said uncertainly.

'Am I?'

She blushed deeply. 'I'm sorry for what happened just now—'

'Forget it—start again,' he encouraged, enjoying the sight of her blue eyes blazing as she assured him she would. 'You've got five hungry men to feed.'

Her eyes flickered as she glanced at his friends. Her expression said she had forgotten them.

He could hardly blame her for that, when so had he.

She started by preparing a fresh tray of canapés—something fast and delicious—and was stunned when Mac joined her at the stove. The space was small and he took up most of it. He was cool and she was hot. She picked up the tray and gripped it tightly so he couldn't see her hands were shaking.

'Don't bother warming them up.'

'It will only take a minute and I promise you they'll taste better.' Confident where her food was concerned, she only wished that confidence could stretch into her everyday life—if it had she might even have been able to hold the stare of a man to whom disagreement was clearly something new, and humour his constant companion. 'I'll just flash them under the grill,' she told him in her most professional voice. 'Excuse me, please.'

He stood back.

But he was too quick for her and stole one off the tray, biting into it with relish.

'These get better when they're warm?' he demanded with surprise.

'Yes, they do taste better warm,' she assured him, growing enough in confidence to block his route to the grill before he could eat the rest. The desire to please him was dangerously strong. The sight of his sweeping ebony brows rising in genuine appreciation for her food was like receiving an award ten times over. Plus she was relieved. She had a suspicion that if she failed to please Mac his authority over the other men would leave her with an empty chalet.

'So, tell me how you made them,' he demanded, aiming that disturbingly intense green gaze into her eyes.

'You want the recipe?'

His face creased in a devastating smile. 'I'll get one of my chefs to make them for me.'

Of course. She should have known that. Nothing in her life could have prepared her for this, Lucy realised. Mac was no ordinary guest and however friendly he might appear it was time to rein back and put everything on a professional footing. 'Tiny circles of toasted Bruschetta topped with goat's cheese,' she recited firmly, clinging to her one area of expertise, 'finished with a slice of fresh fig and a drizzle of honey. And I promise you they're even better when they're heated up,' she said, gaining in confidence.

'Aren't most things?' he murmured close to her ear before moving away.

She needed a moment. She couldn't play these games. In a few words Mac had succeeded in turning her body into liquid fire. He was a playboy and she was an unsophisticated cook—she had none of the know-how. She never flirted with guests, and that short bout with Mac had left her reeling. That he was a player, she had no doubt. That he was playing with her, she had no doubt either. Women were a game for men like Mac, and he was way out of her league. The only way she could survive the week with her self-respect intact was to stick religiously to what she knew—which was cooking.

He had only been here five minutes and he was already suffering from a painful bout of sexual frustration made worse by noticing small things about Lucy—such as she was very tidy, very precise and very contained; the latter was in itself a challenge.

He shouldn't be noticing her at all, he told himself sternly, trying to pay attention to a conversation between his friends about stocks and bonds that would normally have held him riveted. For some reason, watching Lucy loading a clean china platter with perfectly warmed canapés prior to handing them round was far more interesting—possibly because her hands were small-boned and pale, and yet her fingers were flexible and strong, and the thought of those hands touching him was…intriguing.

He liked her. He snapped a response when one of his friends tried to draw him into their conversation, and then she caught him looking at her and coloured up. He liked that too.

It was a relief when Lucy redeemed herself with an excellent meal. Her lush curves pleased him and he didn't want to replace her with some fashionably thin creature whose only goal was to get a trophy lover in her bed. Where was the challenge in that?

Then Lucy mentioned cheese and everyone groaned.

She flushed with embarrassment and both the desire to defend her and the pressure in his groin increased.

'My apologies for feeding you too much—'

'Too well,' he corrected her.

Her swift intake of breath brought on another surge of interest from parts of him that were now refusing to be ignored.

Her face brightened. 'Then shall we eat French-style tomorrow?' she suggested, full of innocent delight to think her menu had gone down so well. 'I mean, cheese before pudding,' she said, visibly paling as he stared at her. 'If that's all right with you…?'

His lips quirked, but he kept a commendably straight face. 'We're in your hands,' he assured her, matching her stare for stare.

Her cheeks were flaming. What was happening? Her life had been straightforward up to tonight. She worked in the background cooking and never connected with a guest. Not that she was connecting with Mac—she didn't flatter herself to that extent. But it was impossible to ignore him—impossible to forget what she'd seen when she'd been on her knees in front of him at eye level with his crotch. Now he was suggesting he was in her hands… How was her imagination supposed to deal with that?

It was no use wishing that she were better looking, or more sophisticated, or that the right words might sometimes come smoothly to her lips. But just because she was quiet and good and plain, didn't mean she lacked outrageous thoughts. Those thoughts ranged a lot further than serving Mac cheese.

She refocused as Tom left the table. 'You're an excellent chef, Lucy.'

'Thank you. Whatever you prepare for us, and in which-ever order you choose to serve it.' Tom went on, 'I, for one, shall certainly relish every mouthful—'

'As shall we all,' Mac cut across him sharply in a tone that startled her. He stepped in front of her, shielding her from the other men. 'There will be three types of canapés tomorrow,' she promised hectically, desperate to return to safer ground. 'And none of them broken.'

The men laughed, and to Lucy's relief Mac relaxed too. She laughed along with them, but her laughter sounded strained. Mac was still close by and her body insisted on reacting violently to him. Her nipples were erect, and another, far more intimate part of her was swelling so in-sistently a man like Mac, so sexual and knowing, must surely know…

She was so wrapped up in these thoughts she barely noticed the other men thanking her, and one by one, leaving her alone with Mac.

'Three types of canapés, and some really good cheese? That sounds good to me,' Mac commented approvingly.

His voice pierced her trance. Now the meal was over her confidence was stripped away. 'It's not a problem,' she said, hoping Mac would leave her to it as she glanced at the deserted dinner table. 'Just let me know what else you'd like and I'm sure I can handle it.' She was thinking of recipes—he was clearly not.

'I'm sure you can,' he agreed, resting back against the wall.

CHAPTER THREE

DID Mac have to be so attractive when he smiled that lazy smile with his green eyes glinting? She was the last person on earth who knew how to deal with a man like that, Lucy told herself sensibly as she served the men lunch the next day. It wasn't just Mac's fierce looks, which set him apart in a world of bland, but the sexual energy he exuded. If she got too close to that she'd get scorched. She only had to glance in the mirror to know he wouldn't be attracted to her.

'Do you want me to help you clear the table?'

'No,' she exclaimed, feeling awakward. Mac's smile was confident and sexy as he leaned back against the wall.

She was in a hurry to finish cleaning up. She had a date tonight. The honour of the chalet company was at stake. Her colleagues swore this was something only she could do for them.

'Do you have some special routine you follow?' Mac said, breaking into these thoughts. 'Lucy?'

'Rinse and stack?' she said hopefully, glancing at the dishwasher. She could do with some help.

Mac's lips pressed down in wry approval. 'Don't let me stop you.'

She was still open-mouthed when one of his friends poked his head round the door.

There was a moment of complete stillness as he took in the scene and then spoke to Mac. 'We thought we might take a walk into town.'

Lucy breathed a sigh of relief.

'Fine,' Mac said, without breaking eye contact with her for a moment. 'You go right ahead.'

He was staying with her?

He wanted to stay with Lucy. He wanted to know why she was in such a hurry, and why, when she had just served another fantastic meal, she was still lacking in confidence. Lucy wasn't good at her job, she was out-standing—so why the angst?

'Don't you want to go into town?' she hinted.

'I'm in no hurry.'

He didn't have to give Lucy a reason for staying in a chalet he owned. If he had he might have said he didn't want her bolting while he was gone. The last thing he wanted was to have to replace her with some sex-starved Seasonnaire. But that was only part of the truth. The novelty of a quiet, self-effacing girl attracted him. She tried so hard, and had overcome the problems quickly and efficiently. He wanted her to grow in self-belief. He wanted to hear this quiet girl scream with pleasure when she lost control in bed.

She'd never had this much scrutiny from anyone, but with her calm head on she could understand that Mac would want to be sure she could hold things together for the week—though he could ring head office and have her replaced at once if he wasn't satisfied with her work. Would that be too easy for him? He didn't look like a man who embraced easy.

Dragging her thoughts from Mac, Lucy turned with relief to rinsing plates. But he was still there in her head. Mac with his glossy black hair and fabulous emerald eyes—Mac steeped in pure, potent power—Mac who unnerved her—deliciously. *Unnerved her?* She was completely out of sync.

'Lucy?'

'Yes?' Her guilty gaze flew to Mac's face.

'You seem…distracted?' he probed.

'Distracted?' She gave a nervous laugh. 'No… I was just planning tonight's meal.'

'Do you like the uniform?' Mac enquired as she fiddled with it.

'Yes, I do.' She met his gaze, determined not to be put off her stroke. She didn't wear the uniform with the same flair as, say, Fiona, but at least it made her feel anonymous and safe. 'I feel…like I belong,' she added as an afterthought, undoing her apron now they'd finished clearing up.

She had turned away to hang her apron on the peg behind the door and so she didn't see Mac frown.

Then Tom came back to have another go at persuading Mac to go with him into town.

'I'll leave Omar here should you need anything.'

'No, take him too,' Lucy told Mac, thinking the invisible presence of a bodyguard she might stumble across at any moment almost as alarming as having Omar's boss scrutinise her every move. 'There are people on call at the chalet company if I need anything.'

'In that case, see you later, Lucy.'

'My pleasure,' she added to an already empty room. If she had needed a reality check on how vital she was to Mac's existence, she just got it.

As the front door shut behind the men she sank down on the nearest chair. She was trembling. She felt as if she'd run a marathon. She had. She had just completed the most important race of her life—to keep her job, though she wasn't foolish enough to think that couldn't change at any moment if Mac changed his mind.

She had to get back to work. Dreaming didn't clean floors—plus she had some eggs to beat for tonight's meal before covering them and leaving them in the fridge…

Staring round the gleaming kitchen as she cracked eggs in a bowl on autopilot, Lucy mulled over what she had learned about her guests. Aside from an overload of testosterone in the chalet, there were a lot of heavy gold rings in evidence engraved with family crests. Theo didn't wear one, but Tom's crest, along with Sheridan's and William's, marked them out as members of the British aristocracy. That was simple enough to work out, but what was she supposed to make of the fierce lion and the scimitar engraved on Mac's ring?

The vision of an awe-inspiring desert landscape came to mind. But where had the green eyes come from? And such eyes…eyes that spoke of billowing Bedouin tents and the pearly light of dawn on the oasis as lovers woke and stretched their pliant limbs before making love again and again and again…

It took remarkably little imagination to take the hunk in jeans and place him in flowing robes. Hmm. Whisk suspended. As the picture drew clearer the whisk picked up pace again. The silk sheets on their Bedouin cushions would cling tenaciously to Mac's powerful limbs, hinting at the brute strength underneath. But the sheets were covering him.

So she'd throw them off.

'Are you going to beat that egg to death?'

She nearly hit the ceiling as Mac stopped her hand. She hadn't realised he'd come back.

'What has that poor egg done to you?' He held her gaze in the most disturbing fashion.

'I was just surprised when you came back.'

'Is there a curfew in operation?'

'Sorry.' Her brain was addled. Mac in cool black performance gear, ready for the snow, was even more alarming than Mac in jeans. And he was still holding on to her hand.

'Don't look so worried,' he said, releasing her. 'I'm not checking up on you.'

Then why was he here? Lucy nursed her hand. Mac's touch was warm, firm and commanding—and he'd let go of her far too fast for her daydreams and not nearly fast enough for here and now.

'So, what are you up to?' he said, staring into her eyes.

She gazed around, desperate for an answer. 'Something for tonight…cake.'

'Cake?' Mac prompted, staring pointedly at the array of cakes already laid out on the table.

'Isn't Tom waiting for you?' Lucy said hopefully.

'And if he is?'

'Could you pass me the cake tin, please?'

He held it out. She took hold of it, but he didn't let go, so now she was joined to Mac by an inflexible ring of tin.

'Lucy?'

She blinked and returned to her customary kitchen-confident self. 'If you'd like a piece of the cake I've already made, just sit down, and I'll—'

'Serve me?' Mac suggested wickedly, releasing the tin.

'I'll cut the cake,' Lucy said primly, reaching for a knife.

'I've changed my mind,' Mac told her, and with one last mocking stare, he left the room.

Mac might have left the room, but he hadn't left her thoughts. He was very much part of them and doing things to her that were almost certainly forbidden by law in several countries. How not to long for that? Running through a list of ingredients for the next meal didn't come close.

CHAPTER FOUR

LUCY spent the next hour in her small attic room, pacing up and down. If only plain girls could be born with a lust bypass, she reflected, pausing by the mirror to view her unchanged reflection, it would make life and rejection so much easier for her. Of course, she knew her relationship with Mac was purely professional, and she'd only known him five minutes, but it would have been nice if, only for a few moments of that time, the frisson she felt could have been a two-way connection. The best thing now was to have a long soak and try to forget him. But she couldn't, because she had somewhere to be and there were jobs to do first—beds to turn down, bathrooms to clean, towels to check, fires to bank up…

She was running late by the time she finished all her remaining tasks and she still had to get ready—number one on the list was a quick bath, and then she'd have to run all the way to the club where her friends would be waiting for her.

Interest laced with concern for Lucy had developed into hot, shameless lust. Razi had to have her. She was beautiful, unaffected and available—and as soon as he had given her a chance to clear up the chalet and set up for the morning he was going to have her.

His impatience was easy to explain—apart from the ache in his groin the clock was ticking. He had never felt the weight of duty more. He embraced the responsibilities coming his way with enthusiasm, but was under no illusion as to the effect they would have on his lifestyle. A traditional marriage—even if not to his cousin Leila—was on the cards. He owed it to his country. But before then…

'Preoccupied, Razi?' Tom asked him discreetly.

'You know,' he said offhandedly. They were sitting in a noisy bar and he was already itching to move on. The drinks weren't cold enough and the nibbles tasted of cardboard after Lucy's delicacies.

Next time she could serve them on her naked body and he'd lick the champagne she spilled off her belly.

'We can move on if you like,' Tom suggested.

'Sorry, Tom. Didn't mean to ignore you—things on my mind.'

'Oh, no.' Tom sighed theatrically and passed a hand across his eyes. 'Let me guess.'

'Don't,' he said sharply. For some reason he couldn't stand the thought of anyone, even Tom, making sport of Lucy. 'Don't even go there, Tom. Let's just move on.'

Muffled up in a super-sized ski jacket, a long scarf, a woolly hat with a bobble on top and a thick pair of gloves, Lucy hurried along the empty streets towards the club. The streets were deserted because everyone was already cosy and warm inside one of the many restaurants and bars by this time of night. It was a world of muffled music and the occasional blast of noise and laughter as a door opened briefly.

She was feeling guilty as she scudded along, knowing her brothers would have loved an event like the one she was due to take part in, while she felt shy at the prospect of entering a crowded club where everyone would know each other. She only hoped she could find her colleagues straight away when she arrived—and that Mac and co didn't decide to go there too. She shivered at the thought of it and almost lost her nerve and turned around.

Her enthusiasm for the event shrank even more when a member of a rival chalet company barred her way at the entrance. 'Here's the runner up,' he announced to his friends, who all started laughing. She hurried past, but her confidence had taken a dive. It got worse when she saw all her colleagues waiting for her and looking so hopeful.

'Ready?' they chorused.

'As I'll ever be,' Lucy confirmed, wondering why she had agreed to sing in the first place. Being a good choir girl hardly qualified her for the annual karaoke competition between the rival chalet companies, and the moment she entered the makeshift dressing room, which doubled as the ladies' restroom, she knew she'd made a big mistake. She didn't have the personality for something like this.

'Make-up?' one of the girls prompted, waking her out of the terror stupor. They were stripping off her coat and scarf, and one of them plucked the hat from her head.

'I don't have any make-up.'

'You don't?' The girls looked at each other in alarm.

'I've never bought any.'

Alarm was replaced by incredulity.

'I'm not very good with it.'

'Not surprising if you never tried,' one girl said with an encouraging smile, stepping forward. 'No worries—we'll do it for you.'

'Oh, no, thank you—but if I wear make up, I'll look awful.' I look bad enough already, Lucy thought, gazing in despair at her reflection. Compared to the other girls she was a real plain Jane.

'You couldn't possibly look awful,' one of the other girls said kindly.

'I only took off my apron five minutes ago.'

'So imagine the transformation.'

They were all so eager to help. How could she let them down? She dragged her confidence cloak tightly round her. 'Okay, I suppose we'd better get on with it.'

Hasty words, Lucy realised as one of them produced a costume for her to wear with a flourish, carolling, 'Ta da!'

'No,' she said firmly. Singing was one thing, but she was going to wear her sensible off-duty clothes, which comprised jeans and a pale blue fleece.

The girls looked at each other and then, recognising the straw that might well break the camel's back, they gave in.

'Just tell me when I have to sing and I'll be fine.' Or she might be, if her upper lip didn't feel as if it were superglued to her teeth.

'Here, have a drink of water,' one of her colleagues said as Lucy licked to no effect with a bone-dry tongue.

Then they all went silent as the contestant from the opposing chalet company began to sing.

'He's got a great voice,' Lucy commented, swallowing hard.

'And he's hot,' one of the girls added.

Better to know she didn't stand a chance before she headed for the makeshift stage, Lucy reasoned. 'I'm going to give it everything I've got.' She smiled bravely as a pile of make-up bags hit the counter.

Then the girls took over, transforming her while she could only watch helplessly. One of them brushed out her hair and curled it with a heated wand, while another made up her face.

'Relax—I do this as a living when I'm not doing the ski season,' one girl assured Lucy as she applied a brown stripe beneath Lucy's cheekbones, a white one above and a blob of red on the apple of her cheek.

Now she looked like a painted doll with exaggerated colouring. She should never have let this happen.

Lucy closed her eyes, resigned to her fate, so it was a surprise when she opened them to find that once the stripes had been blended in she didn't look half bad. Her skin looked even, radiant, and her face sculpted. The make-up was like a mask, Lucy realised with relief—a mask to hide behind. Careful work on her eyes and lips had turned her into someone she hardly recognised and Mac would certainly never recognise her if he decided to come in for a drink. 'I had no idea,' she murmured, leaning forward.

'No time for that,' the girls insisted as she continued to stare into the mirror, amazed at her reflection. Taking hold of her on either side, they ushered her outside.

One last glance confirmed the surprising fact that, left loose, her hair didn't look half bad either. Thanks to the styling wand it hung in thick waves almost to her waist. She had never worn her hair like this before, because her mother said long hair was untidy, and, of course, in a professional kitchen her hair was always covered. Make-up? She pressed her rouged lips together anxiously—she'd never get used to it, but at least the girls looked pleased.

'You look amazing,' one of them assured her and they all agreed.

'Amazingly silly?'

'No!'

'Have some confidence,' one girl insisted. 'You won our award when you least expected it, and now you're going to win this.'

'If I could sing better.'

'It's karaoke, Lucy.' They all laughed. 'You're not supposed to sing—just get into the spirit of it and you'll be fine.'

'And if you're not, we'll hide and pretend not to know you,' another girl teased her.

They had left the bar and headed back to the chalet for their skis to satisfy Razi's whim to expend a small part of his energy skiing down the black slope with just the ultra-lights on their helmets to show them the way. With precipices on either side and at the speeds they travelled it was like playing Russian roulette with a loaded gun that had no bullets missing. It was both exhilarating and dangerous. Irresponsible, maybe, but it had left him on a high. The five of them had been doing this since school when they had first climbed out of a chalet window at midnight, leaving the school masters on the trip snoring. These days Razi pleased himself. He owned the chalet and could leave by the front door, but the thrill had not diminished.

They were all down safely, but with adrenalin surging through his veins he still had energy to burn.

'Champagne?' Theo suggested.

'Lead me to it,' Razi agreed, snapping off his skis in anticipation of a short stroll to his favourite bar.

'Do you think we could drop by the chalet? Let Lucy

know what we're up to? Invite her along?' Tom questioned with a knowing wink.

As Razi might have anticipated, this drew comment from the other men. They were experienced men of the world, but they had all seen something in Lucy—just as he had. His hackles rose. 'Lay off her, boys,' he warned, lifting off his helmet. 'You could all see Lucy was overwhelmed when we rocked up.'

This drew a second chorus of knowing smirks, which he ignored. 'The least we can do is give her a chance to get used to us.'

'To you, don't you mean?'

He refused to dignify Theo's comment with a reply.

Tom drew alongside him to observe discreetly, 'That's extremely thoughtful of you…'

'It's nothing.' Razi dismissed the comment with an impatient gesture. 'Lucy was fine when we left and she's probably asleep by now. She also left food on the table at the chalet, so if we need anything to eat later we can rustle up something for ourselves.'

'Just like the old days,' Theo agreed, coming up on his other side.

Not at all like the old days, Razi's exchange of glances with Tom confirmed. This trip was not the same as the trips they had enjoyed in their carefree teenage years, but the briefest of stops before the weight of responsibility tied each one of them in their different ways. But for all their machismo they were up to the task, Razi concluded, taking a look around his friends. 'Last one to the bar buys the drinks.'

Impossible to imagine their fortunes could be counted in billions as the four friends jostled and wrestled their way across the piste.

* * *

Okay, so this was it. But she needed an urgent trip to the ladies' room first...

'No looking back,' the girls warned Lucy as they accompanied her to the stage.

'I feel sick.'

'There's a fire bucket in the wings,' one of the girls pointed out helpfully.

'I can't remember the words.'

'You don't have to remember the words,' the girls reminded her in chorus. 'This is karaoke, Luce.'

'What if I can't see the screen?'

'We'll sing along with you.'

'What if I can't hear you?'

'You'll hear us,' they promised.

The compére was already on stage, waiting for the crowd to quieten so he could introduce Lucy. Would they ever quieten enough to hear her? It seemed unlikely, thank goodness. Freeing herself from her supporters, Lucy stepped reluctantly up to the red curtain someone had hastily drawn across the makeshift stage and peered through. She couldn't see anything; the light was so bright—much better backstage in the dark where no one could see her. 'Couldn't I sing from back here?'

'That's a no, then,' Lucy muttered as her friends exclaimed in protest.

She wished the spotlights weren't quite so bright, or so well aimed. She felt nervous, hot and scared—and desperate not to let the side down.

'There is one positive.'

'A positive?' the girls encouraged as she fought for breath.

'Yes, I can't make out any faces in the crowd—I took

out my contact lenses,' she managed on a gasp, breathing deeply into lungs that seemed suddenly on fire.

All she could hear now were whistles, shouts and catcalls. The compére had succeeded in whipping the crowd up to fever pitch just in time for her appearance. Great. The position of the fire bucket had never held such colossal significance.

'You'll be all right once you get on stage,' the girls assured her, hands poised on Lucy's shoulders in readiness to push her on.

She didn't have time to think about it. Blundering through the curtain, she was instantly deafened by the booming bass on the backing track and blinded by the lights. She put up her arm to shield her eyes and in doing so missed the introduction. The crowd was silent like a fierce beast preparing to pounce and rip her into shreds, while she stood curled in a protective huddle in the middle of the stage, spotlights illuminating her humiliation, while her backing track moved inexorably on.

Somewhere in the distance she heard the girls shouting her name…

It was no good. She couldn't do it—not even for them. Blinking like a mole, she realised with horror that she couldn't see or hear anything, let alone sing…

Clenching her fists with determination, she forced herself to make a tremulous start, and no one was more surprised than Lucy when her voice gradually gained in confidence and strengthened as the beauty of the melody overpowered her fears. She had insisted on singing a love song when everyone had begged her to sing an upbeat number, and, what with the poignancy of the words and the beauty of the music, she only had to imagine Mac and she was away.

She would never have believed she could enjoy herself so much on stage—even the crowd had silenced in appreciation. They'd gathered round her and many of them were arm in arm as they stared up at her, listening. Discovering she could lose herself in music was a magical experience… Thinking about Mac made it perfect.

CHAPTER FIVE

WHAT the hell?

As they entered the bar Razi's gaze was immediately drawn to the stage where Lucy was singing.

Lucy was singing?

He couldn't believe his eyes, though he'd have known her anywhere. But this was a very different Lucy. Her hair was a shimmering curtain of gold, hanging to her waist, and she was wearing make-up that enhanced her features without being too heavy. Her top was something blue and soft that framed her face and set off the lustre of her hair, but it was her singing voice that really captivated him—as it had every other man in the room.

His expression darkened as he took in all the other male onlookers lusting after Lucy. Her singing and the sincerity of her interpretation had them gripped. Her voice was richly seductive and as beautiful as if it came from her very soul. It was also the husky tone he had imagined hearing in bed…

There was a solid mass of bodies at front of the stage between him and Lucy, but it parted for him like the Red Sea. He didn't even have to elbow his way through. His motors were running and everyone knew it. No one cared to get in his way. She had finished her song and the audience was demanding an encore. Men were cheering and wolf-whistling as he reached the front, by which time she was singing again. The fact that that they found her pleasing was irrelevant to him—or maybe even made it worse. His warrior ancestry pressed down on him. The fact that he adored women demanded action. For however short a time Lucy Tennant was his to protect and defend—

And make love to, he added silently as she stared at him in alarm.

Her voice faltered. The audience fell silent. The tension mounted. He sensed a tipping moment when the crowd would either cheer her to the rafters or boo her off the stage. Her eyes locked with his in silent appeal.

For one fire-burst moment she was so high on adrenalin she exulted in the fact that Mac was staring at her. She had been persuaded to sing an encore, but she wanted to sing for Mac—so he could see who she could be and hear what she could never hope to express in words. This was Lucy Tennant flying high and wide, allowing the music to speak for her. Singing made anything possible…

Or would have done, had not Mac's eyes been narrowed. With disapproval? It was hard to tell. He was looking at her—the audience was looking at him—and then at her. And back to Mac. Their little drama was proving far more interesting than the karaoke competition and she could hardly ignore him. Slowly but surely all her confidence-inspiring adrenalin seeped away, and then everything spiralled in. What was she doing singing on a stage—other than looking ridiculous?

But then the incredible happened. Mac's face changed, relaxed. His eyes darkened as he stared at her and his mouth slowly curved in a sexy smile. Was that a nod of approval? Was it? Mac wanted her to sing for him and that was what she was going to do.

The moment she started singing again everyone began to cheer. They were on their feet applauding her—a noisy frame to the stillness that had developed between her and Mac. By the time she had finished the song, she was oblivious to the cheers. She was trembling all over, her brain in a whirl of confusion. How amazing that moment of connection between them had felt! Mac's power... His reaction to her singing... Her reaction to him... Arousal... Frustration... Overwhelming relief...

Mostly relief, Lucy realised now she was coming back down to earth. A few more seconds on stage without Mac willing her on and she might have turned into her usual bashful self—and for a crowd fuelled up on drink and excitement that wouldn't have worked.

Now she'd won. Incredibly, she'd won. She laughed, shaking her head in disbelief as her friends crowded to the front of the stage. Mac stood at the side at the foot of the steps, quietly waiting for her. That was perhaps the sexiest, the most telling moment of all. They had to call her name twice she was so distracted by him, and on the second time of calling her Mac looked up, his face creasing in the familiar bad-boy smile as he slowly began to applaud without ever once losing eye contact with her. 'Go on,' he mouthed. 'You won...'

Still shaking her head, she walked forward to accept her prize.

'I don't know why you find it so surprising,' Mac said, offering her his hand to help her down the steps at the side of the stage. 'You have a great voice, Lucy—and a great way of putting a song across.' He shrugged, muscles easing across the wide spread of his shoulders as he stared down at her with humour in his eyes.

'You're still here,' she said foolishly, all her shyness returning in a rush. Being on stage was one thing—being here in front of Mac with no spotlights between them was something else.

'Of course I'm still here,' he said as if she'd said something very puzzling indeed. 'Why would I go?'

Breathing was hard suddenly. She could think of a million reasons why he would go, but she wasn't going to give him any hints. Instead she forced a laugh, knowing he had to be joking. Mac was a guest and she was a chalet girl. He didn't want her—not in that way.

'Drink?' he suggested. 'Or back to the chalet?'

She blinked, refocusing in a rush. There was no mistaking his meaning. Even she wasn't naïve enough for that. It was all there in his eyes and in Mac's body language. It didn't come much more direct. His eyes spoke of sensual promise. There could be no misunderstanding. And, of course, she should rebuff, rebel, refuse—and to hell with the fact that Mac was a guest and she mustn't offend him—

But there was a small problem with that. She wanted him. She was violently aroused.

Mac's compelling gaze didn't waver from her face for a single moment, and suddenly the thought that he might want her back at the chalet to clear out the cinders or coddle him an egg seemed far more ridiculous than the realisation that he wanted her in bed. Mac, in casual clothes that moulded his powerful frame with formidable attention to detail, wanted her.

Mac, who looked as fresh and ready for action as if he

hadn't been thrashing the slopes for the past few hours, wanted her?

He looked lush. Mac was the quintessential forbidden fruit. She would miss out on her taste if she didn't find the courage to seize the moment—and when better than now? She would never get another chance like this one. 'I'd better get my coat.'

'You better had,' he said.

He felt a surge of heat and triumph—not that the final outcome had ever been in any doubt. Lucy had needs and he had urges. It was a match made in…Val d'Isere. It was a match that would last for precisely one night. He'd leave her happy, but he'd leave. His playboy life was over. Duty beckoned and he was ready to serve.

He smiled as she came shyly towards him, all buttoned up and ready to be undressed. He'd serve Lucy Tennant and then he'd serve Isla de Sinnebar with the same focus and energy—though for a lifetime rather than a single night.

By the time they reached the chalet he had extended Lucy's time with him to one night and one day to accommodate all his plans. He enjoyed her company. He loved her voice. She didn't have the slightest idea how beautiful she was. Granted, the outfit she was wearing now was dull, but that only whetted his appetite for unpeeling her. She'd be like a ripe, delicious fruit emerging from layers of tasteless pith, and from what he'd seen of Lucy on stage there was enough sensitivity and passion to keep his interest way beyond a single night. It was just a shame life didn't work that way. However he felt about her and whatever happened between them, duty would always come first for him, but that was no reason not to make the most of the time they had.

The chalet was empty when they got back. Taking off her boots slowly, she could feel herself blushing scarlet, second-guessing his plans. When it came to sex she knew she could only disappoint. What she knew about sex could be written on a pin head and to date Mac had only seen her camouflaged in layers of clothing, but when that came off—

'Are you cold? Shall I run a bath for you?'

She stared at him incredulously. Mac run a bath for her? Shouldn't it be the other way around?

His smile widened. 'Better still, let's use the hot tub together. Don't pretend it hasn't occurred to you.'

Now his arm was round her shoulder and he was leading her up the quaint wooden stairs, past the cosy living room, and on up the next flight of stairs to the main bedrooms, and then up another flight to the master suite on the top floor, which was entirely his.

She was trembling so hard she hardly registered what was happening as he closed the door behind them. Unzipping his jacket, he tugged it off and tossed it aside. 'Your turn,' he said, flashing a glance down the length of her safely bundled-up body.

He wanted to play striptease? 'I want to thank you for not sacking me,' she said primly, clinging with everything she'd got to the one thing that made some sense.

'I don't talk business after six o'clock—it's a rule I have,' he murmured, toying with the toggle on her jacket. 'And I'm still waiting. For you to take it off?' he prompted, angling his chin to direct his amused stare into her eyes.

She supposed that was okay. Unzipping her jacket self-consciously, she hung it neatly on a chair.

Mac flipped the braces off his ski pants and tugged off his top.

She gasped and looked away.

'I'm waiting, Lucy.'

Match that impossibly hard-muscled torso with something he'd find desirable? Match Mac's confidence? She couldn't— She really couldn't—

Mac gave her no chance to nurse her concerns. One minute he was leaning against the wall, looking relaxed, and the next she was in his arms.

'Shy?' he murmured. 'I like that. Though I would never have guessed you were shy after seeing you on stage tonight.' His mouth curved in a wicked grin, only millimetres from her mouth.

'That was a one-off,' she admitted, staring into his eyes.

This was all happening so fast she felt dizzy. But in a good way, Lucy decided. The sensation of being pressed into hard, unyielding muscle was amazing—and would have been even more so without quite so many layers in between. Mac toyed with the zipper on her fleece, sliding it down slowly. All she could think of was his erection, pressing insistently huge and hard against her. To say she was melting with desire was something of an understatement.

'Say something,' he murmured.

'I can't...'

Cupping her buttocks possessively, he smiled. 'You're right—why waste time talking?'

His hands tightened and released until every pleasurable sensation she had ever known in her life was exceeded by infinity. She couldn't stifle a moan or breathe steadily or pretend a moment longer. Every nerve ending in her body was primed and ready—every resolution she had ever made to remain at least pure-ish until The One came along meant nothing. There was no past, no future, there was only this, longing for Mac to make love to her.

As if sensing this change, he took her hand, linking their fingers in a gesture that was both deeply intimate and reassuring. He led her past the king-sized bed she had dressed herself with crisp white sheets, and on towards the doorway leading into the impossibly luxurious bathroom and from there to the deck and the hot tub. She cleaned the area twice a day and knew it well. She had even stood here dreaming, but she had never imagined in her wildest dreams that one day she might use it, let alone make love in it. It was as if she was seeing it all again through new eyes—the exquisite apricot-veined marble that complemented the azure skies and shimmering snow-capped mountains in daylight, now framed in black velvet shimmering with diamond stars. There was an uninterrupted wall of glass overlooking the moonlit mountains, and, as far as she was concerned, it was the most romantic place on earth…

'Second thoughts?' Mac murmured, misunderstanding her silence as she stood gazing out.

'None,' she assured him.

'Do you want to get undressed in the bedroom?' Lifting her hand to his lips, he held her gaze.

She looked so vulnerable she touched some long-forgotten part of him. He had learned to switch his feelings on and off like a light bulb as a boy when it had been the only way to cope with the disappointment of promised visits from a mother who never came to see him. Now he understood his mother had had too much to lose. The ruling sheikh, his father, wouldn't tolerate his mistress having another love interest—even if that love interest was their son. His mother had had to forget him, just as he had learned to forget all the other women who had passed through his life. But Lucy was different—at least, she was for tonight.

The hot tub was bubbling temptingly and steam was rising into the night sky by the time she returned from the bedroom. There was a mountain range of foam waiting for her to step into. He was gazing east towards the Isla de Sinnebar when she pushed the door open and came out to meet him. His heart juddered when he saw her. He was still half naked and his feet were bare, while Lucy was wearing an abundance of duvet in stark white—and still managing to look indescribably lovely to him.

'You won't need the duvet in the hot tub.' He grinned as he held out his hand to take it from her.

She stood her ground, clutching it tightly.

'Have you changed your mind?' He would never force her. 'Do you want me to leave you to it?'

'No need,' she whispered. And taking a deep breath, she dropped the duvet and walked towards him.

Two more paces and she was in his arms.

'Are you going to bathe with your clothes on, Mac?'

He smiled into her eyes. She was so trusting and so beautiful, and just for tonight they were going to live the dream.

She glanced at the glittering foam. 'Shall I undress you?' she suggested shyly. Her voice was shaking.

He smiled down at her. 'Or you could enjoy the hot tub all by yourself.'

She held his gaze with her honest eyes. 'I don't trust myself in all that water without something to hold on to…'

His lips tugged in a grin. 'You have all the answers, don't you?'

'It's work in progress,' she admitted with the truthfulness he loved about her, and then her face grew serious as she no doubt contemplated what was about to happen.

His mood changed too. Pushing the last of his doubts aside, he laced his fingers through her hair and, cupping her head, drew her close to kiss her. Her lips were plump and yielded softly beneath his mouth. Kissing Lucy filled him with feelings he couldn't name—feelings it was better not to name. Sex was what they both wanted and needed, and sex, like skiing, was a sport at which he excelled.

CHAPTER SIX

SHE ran her palms across the wide spread of Mac's shoulders and then down his arms, over muscles that bulged and flexed. His chest was shaded with just the right amount of dark hair that dipped in a V towards the buckle on his belt, below which she knew better than to look. But she couldn't help herself— she should feel, had to feel, for the fastening on his jeans.

'Need some help?'

Yes, she did, but she wasn't about to admit it. Mac's challenging smile, his strong white teeth, his lips, his tongue, promising far too much pleasure—the humour in his eyes, the pressure from his hands—she wanted everything he had to give her. 'No, thank you.' Her heart was pounding. She had to pretend she was up to this when she could hardly breathe. She rested her fingertips lightly on the top of his belt buckle and swallowed deep.

His kiss was still warm on her lips as he backed her towards the hot tub. She was in a daze as she felt the steps behind her heels. 'Aren't you overdressed?' she gasped as Mac nuzzled her neck, oh, so lightly as a prelude to feathering his hands down her naked arms.

'So? If I am undress me.'

Her eyes widened. She had imagined many things in the lonely wilderness of her bed, but never anything as erotic as the heat and humour radiating from Mac. But when he turned serious and started murmuring to her in a language she didn't understand she was a little nervous— Or at least she might have been, but her body spoke in tongues— Mac was telling her what he'd like to do to her and in what order. 'Oh, yes, please…'

She melted into him with a sharp exclamation of excitement. As he brushed a kiss across her neck she felt the promise of so much more, but Mac was in no hurry.

Telling herself she was relieved—that she needed time to handle the sensation of warm hard flesh on naked flesh—she allowed herself to relax against him. Tentatively lifting her arms, she laced her fingers in his hair and felt it spring thick and vital against her palms. This was wonderful. It was all she had ever dreamed of and more. Resting her face against his chest, she inhaled his clean, spicy scent, wanting to use all her senses to print the moment on her mind for ever. *For ever—*

She heard his jeans hit the floor, and shivered to think of him completely naked, but Mac was smiling against her lips, reassuring her. 'Why are you trembling?' he demanded huskily. 'I'm just a man like any other.'

Now who was dreaming?

As he swung her into his arms she basked in his strength and in his care of her. When he lowered her carefully into the hot tub she was ready for him to join her. He stepped in and moved behind her so she could lean against him, and when he wrapped his arms around her, nuzzling her neck as if they were lovers of long standing, she felt complete.

* * *

The combination of red-hot Lucy and warm, silky water was more aphrodisiac than required. He wrapped his legs around her, enjoying her trust as she rested against him, registering the fact that she made him feel warm and centred. More than that, she made him feel at home in a foreign land. That was Lucy's strength, her talent, he decided—the ability to create a haven, a sanctuary, a home. It seemed wrong that when, for the first time in his life, he wanted to progress a relationship, there was no chance with duty hammering on the door. But until then he would continue to drop kisses on her neck and shoulders and murmur words in his own language for the sheer pleasure of hearing her sigh. Kissing Lucy was equal to drowning in pleasure, and it was taking every bit of his control to hold back.

But then he noticed the silver necklace she was wearing and a worm of suspicion twisted in his gut. Was it a gift? If so, from whom?

It was none of his business—

He made it his business. Looping the dainty chain over his finger, he allowed the tiny silver slipper to dangle free. 'Who gave you this?' he murmured in between kissing her.

'I did,' she admitted.

'You gave yourself a Cinderella slipper?'

She shifted in his arms. 'It's not that,' she protested—a little too strongly, he thought. 'It's a reminder that one day I'll wear something other than snow boots.'

He laughed softly, not believing her for a minute as he rasped his stubble lightly across the tender spot at the base of her neck. She laughed too—in between begging him for mercy, but he was touched by what she'd told him. 'Some day your prince will come,' he promised as he dropped more kisses on her neck and shoulders.

What if he'd already come—and she couldn't have him? Lucy thought, starting nervously as Mac cupped her breasts. He had just reminded her that she was inexperienced—far more inexperienced than he had obviously imagined. Mac thought because her breasts were full and silky, along the lines magazines suggested were made to be admired, fondled and adored, she was used to this. If only he knew…

She cried out softly as he abraded the tips of her nipples very lightly with his thumbnails, wondering how she was supposed to remain silent and composed while he was working this sort of magic on her. Her nipples had never been so sensitive, her breasts so full. She was still getting used to the fact that such a level of arousal was even possible—or that such freedom to express how she was feeling inside was possible. She guessed it was because Mac had no inhibitions and he had made her strong—at least for tonight.

Some day her prince would come? He had. But, unfortunately, unlike her dream, he wouldn't stay—and she had to be content with that.

Content while longing was a new concept. Mac had moved from cupping her breasts to mapping the swell of her belly and now her thighs. The longing was rapidly turning into lust. She had grown warm and sleek in the perfumed water and braver than she could ever have imagined. Sinking lower in the water, she allowed her legs to part in idle invitation—so hungry for him she had no inhibitions left. Mac needed no encouragement—he was already there. Holding her in place with one firm hand, he slipped the other hand between her legs. 'What do you want, Lucy?' he murmured wickedly.

'I want you to touch me,' she whispered back.

She could feel him smiling against her shoulder as he interpreted that request with such an advanced skill and understanding of her needs it outstripped anything she had imagined possible. She was aware of nothing outside the sensation building inside her. Her whole mind was focused on it, her whole being depended on it. 'Oh, yes,' she murmured, moving against his hand, feeling the muscles in his chest bunching against her back. 'Don't stop...don't ever stop.'

With a gasp of surprise she came apart in his arms while Mac held her close. She had never known such release, such a fire-burst of sensation. Mac had woken an unsuspected appetite. She arched her body so he had to clasp her breasts and groaned when he played with her nipples and felt them tighten beneath his touch.

Lucy sighed and sought his lips, breathing whimpers of satisfaction into his mouth as he went on caressing her. He loved the sounds that she made—he loved the taste of her—and the scent of Lucy was like a field of wildflowers salted with fresh alpine air and when that was mingled with sultry bath oil it produced something unique and seductive.

His hunger to please her was growing. His hands embraced her buttocks, which felt so soft and warm and yielding beneath the warm foam. He knew just how to tease her until she clung to him, sighing in need. She was perfection. She exceeded every expectation he'd ever had for a woman. He had never thought to find a partner so candid in her needs or so sensual—certainly not one as faultless and innocent as Lucy. As far as he was concerned, she was woman.

As she timidly edged one leg over his he touched her again. Crying his name eagerly, she grabbed hold of him, but he lifted his hand away. 'Wait…' he whispered in her ear, loving the way she quivered just from hearing the suggestions he made. 'You mustn't be so impatient. You'll get it all… Everything you want…' And he knew exactly what that was.

The water rose and fell around them to the rhythm of his hand. Lucy's lips parted to drag in air as she gazed at him in wonder. Her beautiful eyes had darkened almost to black, and this time he was going to hold that gaze and watch her pleasure unfold. She tried everything she knew to hold off, but soon gave way, bucking violently and crying out wildly in abandon as pleasure took her over. The motion of her body stirred the water and it cascaded to the floor, but neither of them realised until she quietened and they looked around—and when they saw the devastation they laughed like naughty children.

He wondered in that moment if he had ever felt closer to any woman. Having never felt close to any woman, this was quite a revelation to him. 'I hope you've got enough towels in store to cope with a flood?' he said, acting stern.

'How about I use your robe,' she suggested cheekily.

'Before you do that you'd better get out of the tub.' Water fell away from his naked body as he stood. Stepping out of the tub, he reached for a towel and beckoned to Lucy. It made him smile to see she was still a little shy to show him her beautiful ripe body, but he had her swathed in the warm towel before she had chance to be embarrassed. Swinging her into his arms, he carried her into the bedroom.

'What now?' she said, a new confidence in her eyes as she smiled up at him.

'Whatever you're thinking—double the amount of pleasure involved.'

His kisses in the bedroom were leading one place only, but even as his hands cupped her buttocks, tilting her, so that the very place she needed his attention was pressed up hard against his erection, he was raging against the fact that in spite of all the power he wielded there was one thing he couldn't change: this first time with Lucy would also be the last. He'd almost decided to stop when she pressed her tiny hands against his chest. 'I can hear your heart beating,' she said, and, falling silent, she rested her face where her hands had been.

He had meant to hold her away, but somehow his hand got tangled in her hair, and then the fever was on them both and their hands were everywhere, while her warm breath bathed his naked body. 'This isn't right,' he murmured, his thoughts on the Isla de Sinnebar and duty—

'Do we have to decide that now?' she whispered.

Cupping her face in his hands, he used his thumbs to keep her exactly where he wanted as he kissed her again, and this time deeply.

Mac was a lithe, dark prince of the night. She felt so strong when he ran his fingertips over her; he'd made her strong. She'd waited for this moment all her life, but had never expected it to come, Lucy realised as Mac protected them both. She stared at his arms, pinned like steel girders either side of her shoulders, and the hard-muscled torso decorated with a single tattoo that matched the emblem on his ring. 'I know you'd never hurt me.'

'You know me so well, already?' he demanded softly.

'No,' she said honestly, 'but I know I can trust you.'

'Then know this too—I would never hurt you.'

'I'm only frightened I'll disappoint you—I've not had much experience—'

'You could never disappoint me.' His lips tugged with amusement. 'Is that it?'

'You don't mind about the experience?'

'You don't need experience. You just leave it all to me.'

She risked a shy smile.

'And you're reassured?'

'I am.' She trusted Mac more than she had ever trusted anyone in her life—and for no reason she could pinpoint that made much sense to her; she just did.

She drew in several sharp breaths as he moved in a tantalising pattern that never quite achieved the desired result. 'Oh, please—I want you so much…'

'And I want you,' he husked, catching inside her at last. 'You have no idea how much.'

'As much as this?' Arcing her hips, she thrust towards him, claiming him.

He sank deep into moist, hot velvet. Knowing how much he was stretching her, he took it slowly, while she gasped, looking at him for confirmation that it would be all right. 'If I'm hurting you, I'll stop—'

'Don't you dare,' she managed, clinging tightly to his shoulders.

'How much would you like?' he demanded softly, teasing her with a kiss.

'All of you. I want all of you.' With a final thrust of her body she enveloped him to the hilt.

Moving inside her was way too much pleasure. He had to say the alphabet backwards and write an imaginary shopping list of all the things he'd like to buy for Lucy just to bolster his legendary self-control—and that was definitely a first. She didn't even attempt to make it easy for him, moving with an enthusiasm that belied her protestations of inexperience. She had a natural talent for sex. She matched his rhythm, adding her own particular twist to what looked destined to become an exhaustive practical examination of the Kama Sutra. Seeing her confidence had grown, he gave her what she wanted. Grasping her hips, he thrust deep and fast until he was forced to muffle her screams of pleasure with a kiss.

She watched him sleeping, wondering if there had ever been a moment of such contentment, or of such wonder and love. Mac didn't curl up on the bed in her protective ball, he sprawled on his back so that his long, muscular limbs took up most of the available space. He looked so beautiful and so peaceful.

She traced the line of his perfectly sculpted lips with her fingertip, pulling her hand away when he sighed and turned his head slightly. Now she could see where the sweep of his eyelashes cast a blue-black shadow on his face. His ebony brows were slightly upturned, like an exotic warrior of the Steppes…or the desert. Wherever he came from, Mac was a stunning-looking man.

As he moved his hand his ring glinted, drawing her

attention to the symbol on it—the same crest as the tattoo on the left side of his chest—over his heart… A shiver gripped her. She could find no reason for it. Everything was good—better than good. After tonight she'd face things differently. Mac had made her feel like a woman, bolder and more decisive. Maybe she couldn't have him in her life long-term, but she would have the legacy of knowing him. Something told her she would never feel like this about anyone again. She just had to accept that one night with Mac was worth a lifetime without him.

Settling back on the pillows, she turned her face to drink him in. 'I love you,' she whispered, wishing there were something more she could say to express what she felt inside. There didn't seem to be words for falling in love within a matter of hours. Love struck like a thunderbolt. 'I love you' was used so often she worried it had lost its currency—certainly in this instance it seemed woefully inadequate. 'I love you,' she whispered again, knowing it could never come close to expressing what she felt for Mac.

CHAPTER SEVEN

BREAKFAST passed in a whirl of activity. What might have flustered some people—everyone wanting something slightly different—eggs poached, fried, scrambled, boiled—wasn't even a blip on Lucy's horizon. The only blip on her horizon was wondering how Mac would react when he saw her outside the bedroom.

It was time to put personal considerations aside and forget the fact that she had fallen in love.

Forget?

Forget. Just for now, at least. Because now it was time to remember how much she loved the mad hustle of preparing good food for hungry skiers as fast as she could so they could get out onto the slopes without time-wasting. She made sure there was always enough hot coffee, enough tea, enough hot chocolate, enough juice, and an endless supply of crusty French bread—and today was one such morning. The chat round the table was boisterous and bright.

Then Mac entered the room. Conversation dropped. Her heart stopped. He'd just showered; his hair was still damp. He looked amazing. Her insides clenched, relaxed, yearned.

A look passed between them. It was nothing more than

that—a look—but it made her thrill. It made everything perfect. She had vowed to behave with reserve and professionalism, but the look they had exchanged changed everything—and they had the rest of the week together…

Her heart was pounding with excitement as she poured coffee. 'Can I get anything else for you?' she asked the men around the table.

'Lucy has to get away,' Mac informed the group. 'She has an important appointment on the slopes this morning.'

Her heart bounced as Mac looked at her. He was going to take her skiing!

'Abu and Omar will clear up,' he said, dictating events. 'You'd better hurry up, Lucy.' His eyes were glinting with humour that only she saw. 'See you later,' he said casually to her.

'Yes, see you later,' she replied, tugging off her apron.

See you later. There was a world of promise contained in those three words and her spirits were soaring as she left the room. *See you later* cleared the mist on her immediate future another day with Mac.

He blazed into the restaurant. Customers halted with soup spoons halfway to their mouths to stare at the impossibly glamorous man who had just walked in in a storm of testosterone and muscle. Lucy knew the owner of the cosy mountain retreat and had been helping out by doing a little serving while she was waiting for Mac, but now she stopped as Mac, oblivious to everyone staring at him, headed straight for her. 'Ready?' he said, flashing a glance at the chef who poked his head round the door.

With arousal thundering through her she was already by his side, waving goodbye to the owner.

'Do you really need to moonlight?' Mac demanded, ushering her towards the pegs where her jacket was hanging and her ski boots were stacked. 'Doesn't the chalet company pay you enough?'

'It's not strictly moonlighting as I don't get paid for working here.'

'You do enough already,' he said, frowning as he held the door for her.

'The owner's a friend.'

'You let people take advantage of your good nature.'

'I'm fine with it, Mac. Honestly, I'm no pushover.'

The humour in his slanted glance made her blush.

They skied down from the restaurant to the first lift. Mac was every bit as good as she thought he'd be—far faster and more confident than she would ever be. She tried to keep up with him and then found it hard to stop. It was quite a collision, but Mac caught her in his arms and didn't even lose his balance slightly. 'Speed demon,' he commented wryly. 'I can see we're going to have some fun.'

Taking in his athletic form, dressed in the latest close-fitting performance gear, Lucy decided that was mainly what she was afraid of.

For the first time that season she managed to catch a tip and fall off the lift as she got off—or she would have done had Mac's awareness and reflexes not been lightning fast. Catching hold of her, he steadied her before she could suffer the ignominy of holding everyone up. 'It happens all the time,' he reassured her. 'Even Tom took a tumble yesterday.'

But there wasn't even a bump in the snow here and she could only blame Mac for distracting her—Mac who was so utterly gorgeous everyone was staring at him to the point where she couldn't understand why he wanted to be with her. Even though they'd slept together it wasn't exactly a holiday romance.

No, it was something more precious than that, she mused contentedly.

'Shall I lead, or would you like to?' he said, snapping her out of the daydream.

'You'd better lead and wait for me at the bottom—I can't ski as well as you.' She doubted few people could.

Mac stared at her, the customary amusement missing from his face. 'I wouldn't dream of leaving you—I'll ride shotgun. Off you go,' he prompted. As he spoke the clouds parted and the sun streamed down, illuminating his face almost as a Hollywood director would reserve the special lighting for the star, Lucy thought, dazzled for a moment.

'Come on, let's get moving. The sun might be shining, but it isn't the desert,' he pointed out.

She laughed too. They were as far away from the desert as she could imagine. But as she was about to start off Mac caught hold of her arm. 'I've got a better idea,' he said. 'Take off your skis.'

'What?' She looked at him in surprise. 'You are joking?'

'I'm perfectly serious. I'll put them in the rack and arrange for them to be collected.'

'And what do I do—slither down the slope on my backside?' It might be faster, Lucy conceded as several people turned to stare at her in amusement.

'Don't you trust me?' Mac murmured, holding her gaze until she blushed.

'You know I do.'

He was remembering how his brother, Ra'id, had done this for him once—though under very different circumstances. He'd been about ten years old, and on his first trip to a ski resort. Eager to show his big brother he could keep up with him, he'd watched Ra'id take the lift up the glacier and had followed him. Ra'id's instincts had saved his life. Sensing his foolish little brother was in trouble on the slope behind him, Ra'id had made a dangerous ascent of a perilous incline to rescue him. The weather had closed in, and it had taken Ra'id almost an hour in blizzard conditions to reach the snow bridge where Razi had been stranded. Even then Ra'id had been all patience, all control. He had checked for injuries, before taking him slowly down the slope to safety, as he would now take Lucy under much happier conditions. 'Take your skis off,' he prompted, seeing Lucy was still hesitating. Taking matters out of her hands, he snapped her bindings open so the skis fell away and she had no choice but to step out of them. He put her skis in the rack by the side of the slope and then beckoned to her. 'Stand on mine.'

'Now I know you're joking.'

His stare didn't waver. 'Come on, my skis are stronger than you know. Come in front of me and rest against me… Closer… Yes, that's right… Lean right into me.'

Was she really doing this?

'Relax, Lucy. Let me do all the work. I'm going to show you what living in the fast lane is like.'

'Please don't,' she said, suddenly anxious on a number of fronts. She'd broken so many of her own rules over the past few days—skiing fast might seem the least of them, but once again she was entirely in Mac's hands.

And that was something new?

Maybe she had invested so much in her feelings for him already she was frightened to invest more…

'I promise you—it's exciting.'

She was tempted. She stared round at him. Exciting? Had Mac got the slightest idea how exciting her life had become since they'd met? She guessed not.

He nuzzled his face close so now they were sharing the same sparkling champagne air. 'Don't be frightened,' he whispered.

She heard the smile in his voice and tried to relax.

'I'm going to take you places you've never been before, and show you what travelling at speed through the mountains should feel like.' With that he tipped her over the edge of the slope and they were off. She shrieked as her stomach flipped. 'Relax,' Mac yelled, tightening his grip on her. 'I won't let you fall.'

They started to build up speed and it gave him a buzz to know Lucy was gaining in confidence with every yard they travelled. Had Ra'id felt like this? That it wasn't so much an inconvenience taking someone he cared for down the slope, but a sacred trust? 'Feeling safer now?' he demanded as they cruised some flatter ground.

'Thanks to you.'

He tried to remember when he'd had so much fun outside the bedroom. Fun was in short supply when women had one eye on his throne and the other on his fortune, and anyway, he had no time to invest in relationships. He felt a hit of anger and frustration at the thought that this trip to the Alps would soon be over. He'd enjoyed keeping Lucy safe—perhaps more than he should have done.

Mac had asked her if she felt safe. She was safe. He kept her safe. With Mac's arms around her and his body moulded tightly to hers, she wasn't skiing, she was flying.

Mac's arms were firm around her waist and his warm

breath was on her neck as he steered her down the slope. She'd only felt closer to him when they'd been making love. As Mac took her into a wide, sweeping turn she even wondered if this was the most erotic experience of her life—out in daylight where everyone could see them moving as one, breathing as one—her body welded to his—feeling his muscles working and hers respond.

The steep descent to the village was over all too soon, and as Mac skied to a halt Lucy realised people were staring at them. Women were smiling; some of them enviously, but all of them a little dreamy-eyed at the most romantic sight they'd seen that day. She was sorry it had ended and wished they could start over when Mac nudged her off his skis.

'So—did I convince you?' he demanded, lifting off his helmet and ruffling his thick, wavy black hair. 'That skiing fast is great?' he prompted, dipping his head to stare at her.

Had it only been an adrenalin rush for Mac? With the sudden blinding force of understanding she knew the warm, pulsing effects of what had been a night of love for her had been sex for him. Mac was everything she wanted and more—and could never have. He was enjoying a brief affair—she had fallen in love.

'I'll take you back,' he said, shouldering his skis.

'Don't you want to meet up with your friends?' She wanted to give him an out and herself space and time to think.

Mac looked at her and frowned, his lips pressing down in his habitual amused expression. 'We're big boys now,' he said, catching hold of her with his free arm. 'Come on,' he insisted, linking arms with her. 'It's time for an early bath.'

And the rest…?

Lucy's heart bounced with joy as Mac put his arms around her and drew her close. She put her arm around him too, like any other couple in the resort, telling herself she worried too much. Maybe.

The rush of being in the mountains, the sheer glory of the scenery and the indescribable joy of being with Mac had left Lucy on the highest peak of the highest high.

'You feel the charge too—don't you?' Mac challenged, nuzzling her cheek as they strode along.

'Maybe,' she admitted playfully, trying and failing to keep the smile off her face.

'You do,' he said confidently.

There was a sense of urgency to their stride—they weren't running exactly, but it was purposeful and heading one place fast. The urge to be together, to be even closer than they'd been on the mountain, had infused both of them with unusual energy. Lucy felt like the most alive person on the planet—sight keener, hearing so acute her own heartbeat was hammering in her ears like a kettledrum, while the scent of Mac, deliciously spicy, clean and warm, filled every part of her with happy anticipation. It was as if every sense she possessed was keenly tuned to Mac's extraordinary energy levels. Surely everyone knew… They were attracting glances, as if the sexual bond that joined them was a palpable thing. She glanced up at Mac and saw the set of his jaw, the faint tug of his lips, and the look of absolute focus in his eyes. When Mac wanted something he radiated determination. No wonder people were staring at them. Knowing what he wanted—suspecting other people knew about it too—aroused her shamelessly. She wanted to feel like a sexual being, to be desired, to be…necessary.

'We're here,' she said a little self-consciously when they reached the chalet.

'What do you know,' Mac teased, opening the door. His eyes were wicked as he stood back to let her inside.

He shut the door behind them and suddenly all the energy that had spread in all directions was cooped up in one small space. The air crackled with electricity, though both of them suddenly took to acting as if it were a normal day. Tension simmered as they shed their boots, took off their jackets and hung them up. They walked upstairs almost at a leisurely pace, as if their feelings towards each other had been mastered. But it was an illusion, and without needing to say a word they both knew it. The sexual cord between them had never been stretched so far or so thin—the explosion had to come. Even the air they breathed seemed saturated with particles of lust that only added to Lucy's arousal.

'We're alone,' Mac murmured when they reached the landing.

'So we are,' she said, wondering if they had time to reach the bedroom.

Mac acted decisively. 'Kitchen,' he husked, backing her down the hall.

'What if someone comes?'

He grinned. 'Someone will.'

By the time he'd shut the door behind them her top was on the floor. One stroke of his hands and her briefs were round her ankles. He freed himself and lifted her, practically in the same moment.

'Oh, yes,' she gasped, clinging to him as he plunged deep.

Mac stretched her beyond anything she once would have thought possible. The feeling was so far beyond pleasure that to begin with she could only let him take her with firm, deep strokes, while she did nothing but enjoy, but then the urgent need for release overcame her, made her fierce, and she dug her fingers into his shoulders, shouting his name and rocking furiously while Mac pressed back against the door to support her weight. He was hers to please and enjoy. No one could get into the room while she had her legs locked around his waist, and she was beyond caring what anyone heard. They were both brutally aroused, and from here it was a short, fast ride to pleasure and oblivion.

CHAPTER EIGHT

HE LEFT Lucy to take her shower. He kissed her outside her room, brushing silky strands of hair away from her flushed face. For a moment when he released her her eyes were bright with hope, but then she understood. Pressing her lips together, she quietly left him.

He'd stood outside her closed door without moving before taking the stairs two at a time to his own apartment on the top floor. There was no point in wishing things could be different when he was chained to destiny.

Lucy had set the tradition for canapés and an aperitif before dinner. He settled for a coffee and a croissant in town. He chose an anonymous café none of his friends frequented. He needed space. He needed time to think, but whichever way he played it one thing was non-negotiable. He had to make a clean break from everything in his past in order to give his future to Isla de Sinnebar. He shouldn't be thinking about Lucy at all, let alone thinking about her in terms of taking her with him—

Forget it!

He pushed his chair back so violently the other customers turned to stare. He paid the bill and clattered outside in his ski boots to harness himself first to his skis and then to the challenge of the mountains where no troubling personal thoughts could intrude.

But they would.

Lucy already meant more to him than he, in fairness to her, could tell her. She always would. She had won his heart in no time flat, and when it came to things he had to give up to be the type of leader he intended to be, she was turning out to be the biggest sacrifice of all.

She was back in uniform, having showered, dressed and cooked dinner. Tom had asked her to hold everything for an hour as Mac had gone out again to ski. That news only added to everything Mac hadn't said to her outside her room. Fast sex was all part of his race to the finish. She could sense the fact that Mac would be leaving soon, though he was chatting to his friends now he was back as if an aperitif of hot, heavenly sex was an everyday occurrence for him.

Perhaps it was, Lucy reflected, handing round the canapés. Perhaps she was the one who needed a reality check to see those looks he kept flashing her way were just that— concerned looks. He didn't want her burning dinner, after all.

The meal was a triumph, the group of men told her, and now they were going out skiing on the floodlit slopes while she cleared up. 'Have a good time,' she called after them. 'Breakfast at seven?' she confirmed with Mac, acting bright and businesslike as if she weren't hoping for some words of reassurance long before then. He'd changed into jeans, boots and a hooded sweater after taking a shower and looked hot beyond belief, making the gulf between them unbridgeable and herself a fantasist for even imagining it could be any different.

'Are you sure you don't want me to stay and help you clear up?'

She did a double take, while his friends laughed good-naturedly as if this was the most hilarious suggestion Mac had ever made. 'Thank you, I'm good,' she said, smiling a casual smile as if there were nothing between them.

She thought Mac's look was almost one of disappointment, but then he flashed a glance at his watch and his expression firmed up. 'We'd better get going,' he announced to his friends. 'Time's running out.'

She shivered inwardly as Theo clapped a hand round Mac's shoulders as if he understood. They all understood—while, for all her intimacy with Mac, she knew nothing about his private life. 'Have a good night,' she said on autopilot, keeping her smile in place until Mac led the men out of the room.

But then her smile faded. She felt sick, weak, foolish and the rest. Someone should have warned her how much love hurt—she'd have been more careful to avoid it. But she could hardly blame Mac for wanting to ski with his friends when the slopes were floodlit for the torchlit procession down the mountain to the village. Skiing was what he was here for, after all. He was hardly going to stay behind on one of the best nights of the year to help her clean the chalet. Plucking a clean cloth from the drawer, she set to. However many knocks life threw at her she was going to bounce back and start over. The next stage would be to forget him.

Forget Mac? Impossible. She would never forget him. She wouldn't even keep him in her heart as a warning; she'd keep him in her heart because that was where he belonged. And if Mac couldn't see how she felt about him...

He was hardly going to see it now, Lucy reasoned sensibly, giving the table the polish of its life—it was proving harder to bring up a sheen while her tears were falling on it. She didn't need anyone to tell her that Mac would soon be gone, or that she only had herself to blame for falling in love with him, but it was one thing being a fool and quite another knowing it.

'Let me pick up the pieces for you,' Tom offered, ducking his head inside the helicopter.

Pieces? This was a car crash. 'No need, Tom. I've got it covered.' He'd been right thinking Lucy wasn't his usual type of woman, and right again, suspecting he was in too deep. So much for holding back on feelings. Lucy had drawn more feeling out of him than he'd realised he had. She'd given more than he'd ever expected anyone to give—and he had expected no more of Lucy than he expected of any woman.

'Do you want me to pass on any messages?' Tom shouted above the roar of the rotor blades starting up overhead.

It was better to make a clean break—better for Lucy. He'd known his destiny since Ra'id had explained it to him when he was just thirteen. He was going back to Isla de Sinnebar to put on the robes of duty and devote himself to the service of a country. In doing so he would lose his freedom. He did this gladly, but a pure, free spirit like Lucy Tennant deserved something better than a man who had to be so single-minded for the sake of his country.

'Razi?' Tom pressed him as the engine noise increased.

Guilt and longing swept over him. He felt so bad leaving Lucy. The first of many times he would experience such feelings, he suspected as the image of her open, trusting face remained steady in his mind. 'If she needs anything,

anything at all—a job, a reference…' Tom and he were almost as close as brothers and there was no need for explanation—they both knew he was talking about Lucy.

He felt diminished as he handed Tom his no-frills business card. He'd signed it so it carried his authority. 'See she gets this, will you, Tom?' Before Tom had chance to answer or he had chance to change his mind, he gave the signal and the helicopter lifted off.

What was this? She felt sick inside as she sank down on the bed. She had just switched on the bedside light and seen the money someone had left on the nightstand. Before this moment she hadn't even known there was such a thing as a five-hundred-euro note—and now there was a stack of them within touching distance.

Not that she wanted to touch them, even though they were crisp and new and looked as though they hadn't been touched, other than to have whatever paper bands had held them together removed.

There must have been tens of thousands of euros in the neat pile, Lucy realised, staring at them. And there was ice in the pit of her stomach, because she knew. She didn't need it spelling out to her—she didn't need to think about it. Mac hadn't come home with the other men and his bodyguards had gone too. Whoever he was—and she had shut the possibilities out of her mind just to live the fantasy—fabulously wealthy Mac had returned to whatever world he belonged to, leaving her with a small fortune in pinkish, purplish notes, as if sufficient money could paper over the cracks in her heart.

He thought money could do that?

She turned her face to the wall, biting down on the back

of her hand so she wouldn't cry out and the other men wouldn't hear her. Drawing a deep shuddering breath, she told herself she'd got what she'd deserved—a lot more than she'd deserved, in fact; there was enough money here to open her own restaurant…

And even that didn't begin to ward off the chill creeping through her veins. Her legs felt like lead as she dragged them up onto the bed. Tugging up the duvet to her chin, she lay unsleeping, fully clothed and shivering as she contemplated a world that was not just empty now, but irrevocably changed—by Mac's opinion of her, and by his pay-off.

Change was inevitable at the end of the ski season. Change was all-encompassing when a pregnancy test turned out to be positive.

Lucy rested against the wall of her bathroom with her eyes shut. When she opened them again the betraying blue line was still there. She'd been feeling sick every morning recently, and all-over funny—different—changed—as if she weren't alone in her body any longer. There was a very good reason for that, as she now knew for sure…

Stroking her hands down her still-flat stomach, she felt an incredible sense of wonder—instant love—instant fight-to-the-death protective instincts towards the little bud of life sheltering and growing inside her—someone to love—someone she hoped would love her—a family all of her own…

And Mac?

Why did he have to know?

Remembering the pile of money he'd left her and the way he'd left her—leaving Tom to pass on his business card of all things—he didn't deserve to know.

Grit her teeth against the pain as she might, she still

loved him. She would always love Mac. Though she hated what he'd done, she couldn't fight the flood of memories—so many good memories and so few bad—until that last bitter blow, when he'd left the resort without saying goodbye—without leaving a proper message, nothing but that wretched business card that Tom had put in an envelope and sealed. 'You never know when you might need something,' Tom had said in his kindly way, after explaining what the envelope contained.

'I'll never need anything from Mac,' she had assured him tightly, planting the unopened envelope deep in her apron pocket.

'A job, maybe?' Tom had said with a shrug as if he sensed her hurt and wanted to ease it.

'No, nothing,' she had insisted, shaking her head. When she'd returned to her room she had stuffed the envelope to the back of a drawer where it still lay to this day, untouched.

Well, it gave her a use for the stack of untouched bank-notes currently residing in a large padded envelope with her name on it in the company safe, Lucy reflected, throwing away the third pregnancy test she'd done that morning. There was so much to consider. She could hardly arrive at her parents' house with a baby. She would need a home for one—a home with a proper garden where a little girl could play. She was so sure it was a little girl. There was a business to think about. She'd get a job to start with to help with the fund and then she'd strike out on her own.

She was going to be a mother…

The thought had not only filled her with joy, but with renewed ambition. She had someone to fight for now—someone who would need a college fund and a prom dress and every advantage she could give her.

And Mac?

Unfortunately, she had to tell him. She had to relent. She didn't want anything from him, but he should know. Mac should be given the opportunity to know he was going to be a father. She had to give him that chance. She had no choice. Telling him was the right thing to do.

R. Maktabi. CEO Maktabi Communications. Having dived into her sock drawer in a frenzy of 'let's-get-this-over-with', she found that was all that was printed on the card. She almost laughed out loud to think Mac was in the wrong business—communicating was hardly his forte. But there were three telephone numbers: London, New York and somewhere in the Arabian Gulf called Isla de Sinnebar. So that explained Mac's exotic looks, Lucy mused, staring blindly out of the window. Mac had contacts in both east and west and now he had returned to… She shrugged and dialled the London number. Mac wasn't there, a frosty secretary told her. She could practically see the woman flinching over the phone when she'd asked for Mac. She realised now that Mac was an abbreviation of his surname, and guessed not many women used it—or, at least, not to the old battleaxe on the other end of the phone. 'Sorry to have troubled you—'

She drew a blank with New York too—but she'd saved the best 'til last. Closing her eyes, she allowed the vision of a desert encampment complete with billowing ivory silk tents to flow through her mind—and had to stop that thought dead when she discovered how many gorgeous women dressed in rainbow hues like so many lovely butterflies were queuing up to serve canapés to a recumbent Mac, who was reclining on silken cushions as they fed him dainty morsels. That wasn't such a great image.

'An appointment with the CEO of Maktabi Communications?' a very polite man enquired in the softest, creamiest voice Lucy had ever heard when she got through to Mac's office in the Arabian Gulf. 'I'm afraid that won't be possible.'

'But he is there?' She was clutching Mac's card so tightly, she had crumpled it, Lucy realised as she waited for an answer. 'And if he is, may I speak to him, please?' she persisted, remembering who had made her brave. 'It's of the utmost importance.'

'May I enquire what your business is?'

Mac was there. She knew it. She clutched the phone to her chest, her heart hammering so hard she was sure the man could hear it beating in Isla de Sinnebar. She put the phone to her ear again. 'I'm afraid it's personal. Perhaps I could meet with him?' She had no intention of telling some stranger her business—but if she could just get into the building, maybe she could find Mac.

'You cannot possibly make an appointment to see—'

Cannot possibly? She held the phone away from her ear. Was Mac contagious? Had he suddenly become so aloof, so untouchable, he wouldn't speak to people he knew? 'But I know him,' she protested, 'and I'm sure he'll want to speak to me.'

There was silence and then a rather offensive laugh. 'You cannot imagine how many people say the same thing,' the man derided.

How many women? Lucy wondered.

Her heart shrank to the size of a bitter, joyless nut. Suddenly she saw how it must sound—a young girl that no one had heard of rang up to demand an appointment with the head of a large multinational corporation...

'And in any case,' the man rapped dismissively, 'we have a public holiday coming up so there would be no one here to see you. Should you be so foolish enough to decide to come you'll find no one here—everywhere will be shut from—'

'From when?' Lucy demanded eagerly.

'From Thursday,' he said, sounding surprised that she hadn't folded yet.

In three days' time. 'Perfect. Can we arrange our meeting for Wednesday?'

'*Our* meeting?' There was silence as the man absorbed her sleight of hand. 'I don't think you heard me. There can be no meeting, Ms—'

'Miss Tennant—'

'Goodbye, Miss Tennant.'

Lucy stared at the silent receiver in disbelief. How rude. It was another dead end, but she couldn't leave it here. She was shaking and not feeling brave at all after such a humiliating put-down, but with the baby to consider nothing would stop her seeing Mac. Dialling the operator, she got ready to book her flight.

CHAPTER NINE

THE purser on board had just announced they would soon be landing in Isla de Sinnebar. Consumed with curiosity, Lucy stared out of her tiny window as the commercial jet swooped in low over an azure sea. Tiny dots of white marked the passage of sailing boats while a patchwork quilt of ivory, green, gold and tan land stretched away towards distant purple mountains. As the plane banked a city came into view. White spires half hidden in a heat haze. No wonder Mac had an office here. If the rest of Isla de Sinnebar was half as magical as it appeared from the air, he was a lucky man.

A lucky man in so many ways. He was about to become a father. If Mac felt only a fraction of the love she already felt for their baby, he would be the luckiest man alive. She fretted as she thought about it, knowing she could only hope he would love their baby, and only hope that he would make time in his busy working life to see something of their child. He would miss so much if he didn't—and she couldn't wish that on him.

Resolutely, Lucy cleared her mind. It was early morning, and she planned to travel straight to Mac's office from the airport and wait for as long as it took to see him. She had to be businesslike and determined. This wasn't a social call. Her baby's happiness, and, yes, Mac's happiness depended on a successful outcome to this visit. And time was tight. Until she got a new job her savings from the ski season had to be eked out, and, much as she would have liked to, she had allowed no time for sightseeing on the Isla de Sinnebar, and just thirty-six hours for discussions with Mac on the way forward. Her homeward flight was booked in two days' time, just before the public holiday closed everything down.

Dragging her gaze away from the window, Lucy tried to contain her emotions. Fear and apprehension at what lay ahead of her in a country she didn't know competed with her blind faith in what she believed would be Mac's instinctive love for their child. She had to believe he would be thrilled by her news, especially when she reassured him that she was going to take on full parenting responsibility, bringing up their baby as a single mother. But with so little settled it was hard to stop doubt setting in.

She had to concentrate on the positive, she told herself; even on such a short visit she could absorb so many things in a land of eternal sunshine where everything was new to her, but before she could do that she had to change her clothes before the seat belt sign lit up. She had worn a tracksuit for the twelve-hour flight, but had brought a light-weight business suit to wear when she met Mac. She was carrying such momentous news she had left nothing to chance. She must look professional and in control when she met him. She had even run a number of scenarios in her mind to work out how he might react when he heard the news. The only thing she was sure about was that it was important to keep her cool—and in every respect. Her time with Mac was done. She had to face that and get over it. She had a baby to think about now.

Everything ran like clockwork. The airport terminal was a haven of calm, clean efficiency, and the cabs were lined up outside the exit door. Lucy began to relax and to believe that in this sunlit, purposeful country things could only work out well for her.

Everything was so exotic she couldn't stop staring around and had to be reminded with a gentle nudge from a kindly woman standing behind her to move along in the queue. How hard was it to believe that she was here—surrounded by the swish of robes, the click of prayer beads, the faint scent of spice in the air, and the pad of sandalled feet? How could she not feel excited—by the sight of everything around her and the thought of seeing Mac again?

Well… She'd warned herself that he might not exactly welcome her with open arms. And that was before she told him her news. But for now with her heart thundering in her chest she would feast her eyes on his country and, though she might not have long here, she would make the most of every minute so she could tell her baby about it one day.

He had stamped his authority on the kingdom in the first few hours of ascending the Phoenix throne. He had been conducting from the wings as CEO of Maktabi Communications with an office in the capital of Isla de Sinnebar, but now he was firmly established centre stage. The learning curve had been steep for those of his courtiers who were used to the old, lax ways—and for men like his cousin Leila's father, who had imagined the playboy prince would be an easy target when he became King. They should have realised his success in business was founded on his overseeing everything, and that he might be expected to run a country to the benefit of its people in exactly the same way. There would be no sleaze, no corruption, no royal favourites; no exceptions. Even he would have to learn to live within the tight moral structure he had laid out in law. His personal life would be an arid desert until the day he took a wife—and even then he didn't expect love to enter the equation; mutual respect was the most he could expect.

All this activity, along with the eighteen-hour days that accompanied it, should have come as a relief, because it left no time to dream about a young woman who would have been a breath of fresh air amongst all the girls they tried to foist on him now he was the ruling Sheikh. His new powers had encouraged a steady parade of dunderheads with porcelain teeth and falsely inflated bosoms to pay court to him, along with those who had to be dusted down as they were removed from the shelf. When he compared any of them to a girl too honest for her own good and as natural as sunlight, he was tempted to swear off women for life. She might not know it, but Lucy Tennant was as rare a find as a flower in the desert. And like that flower he had carelessly trampled her underfoot.

For Lucy the drive to Maktabi Communications was an education in itself. There was clearly order in Isla de Sinnebar, and a respect for the history and tradition of the ancient land that went as far as a camel lane on the six-lane highway. There was a respect for the environment too. Lucy had yet to see a single piece of litter, or graffiti, and the wide, perfectly constructed roads were lined with vivid banks of flowers.

Flowers in the desert, Lucy mused, settling back in her seat as the cab she'd taken from the airport turned onto a slip road, heading for the city, and one rampant lion waiting somewhere close by. The thought that she was getting closer to Mac with every yard the cab travelled had an inevitability about it that made her quiver with excitement and doubt her own sanity all in the same instant. Instinctively cradling her stomach, she wished she could reassure her baby that this was for the best, and that whatever happened her mother would protect her.

The cab drew to a halt outside one of the buildings with gleaming white spires she'd seen from the air. It was even more magnificent from this perspective, and absolutely huge. Maktabi Communications was written over the entrance, and there was a flagpole outside with a large standard fluttering. Her stomach clenched as she identified the rampant lion and scimitar she had last seen on Mac's ring. How at home that emblem seemed here in this land of power and wealth and glittering exoticism. Now everything made sense about Mac's striking looks. And nothing made sense, Lucy thought, noting the guards on the door. Doormen, she might have expected—but soldiers?

Fortunately, she had changed from the shy, self-effacing girl who, having left the family home, had gained her first lesson in what she could achieve in Monsieur Roulet's kitchen, her main lesson in Val d'Isere and, with the gift of life inside her, had transformed utterly, to the point where she wasn't about to be put off by guards on the door.

'I have an appointment,' she told one of them pleasantly, quoting the name of the man who had so reluctantly spoken to her on the phone. Before the guard even had time to ring through and check she brought out the crumpled card. Mac's card. The card Mac had signed so carelessly before passing it on to Tom,

Thank goodness she'd kept it. It acted like a magic wand. The guard saluted and then reached for the door. He stood stiffly as she walked past him into the vast marble-floored entrance.

Power, Lucy thought, staring up in wonder at an atrium that must have qualified for one of the biggest in the world—if not the biggest. Power was her overriding feeling as she looked around. This whole fabulous white, steel and glass building that Mac called his office thrummed with power. There was a desk at the far end of the lobby manned by immaculately dressed men in white robes and flowing headdresses. Even in her smart suit she felt self-conscious as she click-clacked her way across the marble floor towards them. Everything about the building, including their work station, was low-key and high-tech, while she was too unstylish to be either. But with her baby at the forefront of her mind she was able to explain her business clearly, and after a little wrangle between the two men one of them, with the utmost courtesy, showed her to a low-backed sofa where she was to wait.

And wait.

She visited the restroom twice. She bathed her face in ice-cool water and gazed at her face in the mirror. Nothing had changed. There were dark circles under her eyes, and she looked haggard. She wished she could be one of those effortlessly glamorous people who could wait around and still look as fresh as a daisy, but even at this early stage of pregnancy her energy seemed to be sapped beyond anything she could have anticipated. Of course, it might have helped if she could have something to eat or drink, but she daren't leave her station in the lobby for longer than a few minutes in case she missed Mac.

Having checked at the desk to be sure there wasn't anyone she could see who might bring her one step closer to him, Lucy returned to her seat. There were magazines to read on a low glass table, but she would never have been able to concentrate long enough. The idea had always been to get into the building and then find Mac. She'd been prepared to wait for as long as it took, but could have had no idea she would wait quite so long.

So she'd take this opportunity to set her thoughts in order, Lucy told herself firmly. She wasn't going to give up now. When she'd first arrived and shown Mac's card, one of the men on Reception had seemed impressed and had even stood to greet her, but the other had given him a hard stare and so he had sat down again. She guessed the unhelpful man was the man she had spoken to on the phone. She also deduced that Mac was expected soon and that all she had to do was wait. That Mac was immensely rich had never been in any doubt, but that quite so many barriers would be raised when she tried to see him had been a surprise. Perhaps his company was working on something crucial to the government, Lucy reasoned, glancing at the soldiers outside. Her stomach growled insistently as she studied her surroundings. It was a reminder that she hadn't eaten properly since the previous day and that she had to be more responsible now she was eating for two.

She passed some more time marvelling at a national flag picked out in gold above the reception desk. As she studied the incredible workmanship in the scimitar and rampant lion a wave of quite irrational fear swept over her. It was a struggle to brush it aside, but her imagination was notoriously extreme, and pregnancy hormones were clearly adding to her jumpiness. She glanced at her watch and sighed to see another half an hour had passed. Getting to her feet, she approached the desk.

'My apologies,' the awkward man said insincerely with an elegant flourish of his hands.

'How much longer, do you think?' Lucy said anxiously, feeling a wave of dizziness sweep over her. She glanced back across her luggage sitting forlornly in the lobby. She still had to book into her hotel and didn't want to lose the room.

'That I cannot say,' the man told her with a shrug.

'Then may I wait outside Mac's office, please?'

This garnered a withering look. Lucy's shoulders slumped, but then she tensed, hearing the entrance doors behind her sweep open. There was a guttural cry in Sinnebalese and then a clatter of arms as the guards shot to attention.

Mac had arrived. She didn't need to turn around to know it was him when she could sense him in every fibre of her being.

As the pad of sandalled feet drew closer, and the scent of spice and sandalwood filled the air, her mind cleared, but her body let her down, and just as everything shot into clear focus, all of it making complete sense—the rampant lion—the scimitar—the royal standard—the fact that Mac was not easy-going, sexy Mac at all, but someone else completely—she sank into a faint on the floor at his feet.

CHAPTER TEN

SHE woke in a luxurious bedroom and took account of her surroundings carefully before moving a muscle. It was a large, airy, sumptuous room. A brocade quilt in shades of ivory and gold had been stripped away from the crisp white sheets and folded neatly before being placed on a seat at the end of the very large bed. Blinds had been drawn so that the room was in shade, and at the far end two men were conferring in muted voices. They were both dressed in Arabian robes, but even in the shadows the older man's robes were blindingly white, while the younger, taller, broader, much more imposing individual was wearing robes of royal blue. Of course, Lucy thought hazily, Mac probably had blue blood too.

As full consciousness returned to Lucy everything was instantly clear. Mac was a king. No wonder they wouldn't let her see him. Mac was a sheikh. Mac was the ruling Sheikh of the Isla de Sinnebar. The man she loved was a desert king.

She only had to stir for there to be a change in the room. Without a word being spoken the older man Lucy presumed must be a doctor left Mac's side and closed the door softly behind him, while Mac strode towards her across several acres of exquisitely patterned rugs.

Her world shrank around him. Her heart responded as it always had, with heat and with longing. He stopped a short distance from the bed, with his face in shade. Even though she couldn't see his features clearly she knew immediately that this was not the passionate, easy-going lover she had known in Val d'Isere, but a stranger far removed by rank and dignity from the pitiable aspirations of a kitchen girl.

'Lucy?'

The voice was the same. Mac was the same, and yet he was utterly changed. And not just by a costume, but by the fact he was a king. He had assumed his powers, and with them the weight of duty that had turned his face set and hard. He was looking at her, but she sensed his inner gaze was turned towards a future she could never share.

She had been shrinking back on the pillows, Lucy realised, pulling herself upright. She had to rally for the sake of her baby. She couldn't allow herself to be intimidated by anyone, not even the ruler of Isla de Sinnebar. She must have fainted for want of food and that was unforgivable. She had to be responsible now she was pregnant. She had to think clearly and act for a baby that couldn't act for itself.

The baby wasn't the only reason her body had let her down. When Mac had entered the building her soul had flown to him. That was one part of her that steadfastly refused to accept reality. And perhaps should take a look at him now, Lucy reasoned as Mac surveyed her coldly.

Beneath the lightest of quilts she cradled her belly protectively, glad that whoever had carried her to the bed had at least left her fully dressed, minus her jacket and her shoes. She could see them close by, the jacket hanging on a chair back and her shoes lined up neatly underneath. They were a reminder that she had come here dressed for business and a discussion that would change both their lives. 'Who *are* you?' she murmured. She knew the answer and it was a crazy question, but she had to have her suspicions confirmed.

The man she'd known as Mac shrugged and as he moved his robes swirled, filling the air with the mysterious aromas of Eastern spices. 'My name is Razi al Maktabi. Some of my friends know me as Mac.'

'Razi al Maktabi? Known to the world as His Imperial Majesty, Sheikh Razi al Maktabi of the Isla de Sinnebar?' The implications of this swamped her thinking and her heart raced in terror as the man she'd known as Mac swept into the gracious and traditional Arab acknowledgement.

'Why didn't you tell me?' She hated that her voice sounded so hurt and weak, but she had never been a good actress.

'It never came up.'

No, they'd been too busy making love, or having sex, as Razi al Maktabi must no doubt remember it. It was too late now to curse her blindness, or to remember that even when she'd studied Mac's business card her imagination had failed to extend further than thinking Mac some distant cousin of the ruling Sheikh—if she'd thought about it at all.

The chasm that had always existed between them had just widened to a gulf, Lucy realised, taking in the stern face beneath the flowing headdress. Razi al Maktabi wore the clothes of a king well. The exquisite workmanship of the gold *agal* holding his headdress in place only hinted at the power he wielded, but it was her love for the man that made her heart ache with longing. She had to remind herself she was here for her baby and couldn't be distracted, not even by Mac's fierce glamour.

'What do you want from me, Lucy?'

She sank back on the pillows, speechless. He was so cold towards her. Their time together had meant nothing to him. Mac had closed his mind to ever seeing her again, and yet here she was, stirring up unwanted memories of how easy she'd been, how plain, how infinitely replaceable. She couldn't blame him for thinking she would only be here if she wanted something from him.

She had to leave her feelings aside and concentrate on rescuing something for the sake of their child. Easing her legs over the side of the bed, she tried to stand, but only succeeded in swaying towards him as a second wave of dizziness swept over her. Mac's lightning reflexes prevented her from falling to the ground. But there was such a thing as pride. He had taught her that. Easing her arm from his grip, she felt for the side of the bed and shakily sank down. 'Could you give me a moment, please?'

To his credit, the man she must learn to call Razi stood back as she planted her fists on the mattress, willing herself to be as strong and businesslike as he was. If she was going to finish what she was here to do she had to find strength from somewhere.

'When did you last eat?' he demanded.

She stared up distractedly. 'I can't remember.'

'You can't—' He stopped. 'Fortunately, I ordered broth from the kitchen.' He pointed to a dish on a heated trolley. 'You'd better drink it before we talk.'

There was no warmth in his eyes as he crossed the room to put the dish on a tray. He brought it to the bed where she had intended to turn her head, but pregnancy intervened and she was consumed by ravening hunger.

'Drink,' Razi insisted, standing back. 'I'll wait. You'll feel stronger when you've eaten something.'

She drank the soup greedily, relieved to feel warmth and nourishment flooding her veins. When she looked up to thank him Razi's expression remained unchanged. He was telling her the easy relationship they had shared in Val d'Isere was over and must never be mentioned again, let alone rekindled.

She had barely laid down her spoon before he took the tray away. Having put it down, he turned to face her. 'Why are you here, Lucy?'

Yes, why was she here? Suddenly all the reasons that had seemed so sensible in England appeared ridiculous. She had no idea about the laws governing Isla de Sinnebar, except that the ruling Sheikh held all the power. So where did that leave her? She was the chalet girl Razi had got pregnant on his last holiday before taking the throne. Would he care?

She had to steel herself to see beyond that. There was a child to consider. 'I apologise for arriving uninvited,' she began politely, 'but I had to see you.'

'You had to?' Razi's dark gaze narrowed with suspicion.

He didn't need to tell her the short time they'd shared was over and he had no interest in revisiting any part of it or that they were two strangers who shared no intimacies now. Razi was the all-powerful ruler of a country with much weightier matters to consider than some dalliance with a cook. Would he even be interested in her rights as a mother, or when she told him would he insist on keeping the child and simply dismiss her as superfluous to requirements?

This last thought was so shocking she grasped her throat in anguish and, misreading her gesture, Razi poured her a glass of water. 'You look exhausted,' he said. 'Was it really worth putting yourself through this?'

Yes. A thousand times yes, Lucy thought fiercely, drinking the cooling fluid down. But not for the reasons Razi imagined. He thought she was on some pathetic mission to reawaken his interest in her, which was why he was at such pains to make it clear he didn't want her. Why would he want her when she could only be an embarrassment to him?

'I asked you a question,' he prompted coldly. 'Why are you here? What do you hope to gain from this visit?'

'Gain?' She couldn't think of a single thing other than the knowledge that she had done what she believed to be right by coming to Isla de Sinnebar to tell Razi he was about to become a father, but it was clear from Razi's expression that he took her weak voice for an admission of guilt. 'I don't want anything from you,' she insisted firmly.

'You don't? Really?' he mocked. 'It's a long way to come for nothing, Lucy.'

What could she say to convince him? Lucy wondered as Razi's sweeping brows rose in disbelief. He was a formidable all-powerful sheikh, while she was a rumpled mess, sitting up in bed half dressed, sipping from a glass of water in an attempt to act normally, as if she were strong, as if she were recovering.

He walked across the room to flick a switch and the curtains parted. She recognised the familiar skyline outside and deduced the bedroom was a penthouse suite on top of his office building. There would be staff on call and she had no doubt her time with Razi could be counted in seconds now. The fact that he was here at all was nothing more than a common courtesy he had granted to a member of staff who had passed out at his feet. He could hardly ignore her under those circumstances—he could hardly wait to get away, either. 'Razi—I really must talk to you before you go.'

'I don't believe we have anything to say to each other.'

His stark rebuff showed how misguided she'd been. She had imagined the man she had known as Mac would take a civilised view after a civilised conversation in the sterile confines of his office. Trying to impose her thoughts and wishes on a ruling Sheikh was a hopeless task. Asking him to recall some holiday flirtation with a chalet girl sounded ridiculous, even to her. How could she tell Mac her wonderful news when there was no Mac?

'Are we finished here?' he demanded.

She was hit by panic as he turned to go. 'I don't even know what to call you.'

'Razi or Mac—whatever you like.'

His dismissive gesture suggested it really didn't matter what she called him as she wouldn't be part of his life for very much longer. Mac had seemed appropriate for the sexy guest who, once you got over the shock of his blistering glamour, was at least human, but this man was a warrior king with all that that implied. The desert had always seemed such a romantic place to her, as had the image of a desert king, but the reality was so very different. The desert was a hostile environment and the desert king a stranger. 'Your Majesty,' she called after him.

He spun around to face her at the door. 'Call me Razi.'

With that one command Mac had shed his playboy skin and become Razi the King, a man who was so resolute and inflexible he was as removed from her as if they'd never met. Yet there was something between them. And she had to believe it was more than the memory of what an explosive combination they'd been in bed. There was a real connection between them that she felt more strongly than ever and she refused to believe he didn't feel it too. .

'What do you want?' he said, picking up on these thoughts.

It took all her strength to hold his dark, brooding gaze and not show the love she felt for him, or blurt out the truth for why she'd come in the pointless hope that Razi would relent and soften towards her and that somehow they could cross the barriers dividing them and make this work.

'Do you want a job?'

The question was so unexpected she almost laughed. Not even as his cook—and certainly not as his mistress. Any woman waiting for Razi al Maktabi would truly wait in lonely isolation until and if he found time for her. She had made a huge mistake coming to Isla de Sinnebar, and a second mistake imagining she could reason with this man—but worst of all she had placed her baby in danger, because Razi would never let her go if he knew she was carrying the royal child. Going home must be her aim. The only safe way to tell Razi about their child was from the safety of a lawyer's office.

'Didn't I leave you enough money?'

Lucy sucked in a shocked breath, realising money had never occurred to her.

'How much do you want?' he said, easing away from the door.

Could a man change so much? Lucy wondered, seeing the suspicion in his eyes.

A king would be suspicious of everyone's motives, she

reasoned, but Razi needn't worry, because his money was ring-fenced for her daughter's future. She hadn't touched it. 'I'm not here for your money—though now you mention it—'

'Yes?' His face eased into a cynical smile as if he had been expecting this all along.

'You left me a ridiculous amount of money in Val d'Isere,' she began nervously.

'Have you never received a tip before? I find that hard to believe.'

A tip for good service? Lucy wondered, feeling mortified as Razi's sweeping brows lifted in mocking denial of everything they'd shared. 'A tip? Yes,' she said as her mind cleared. 'Of course.' She borrowed Razi's mannerism and shrugged, as if a guest leaving her a tip big enough to buy a house with was an everyday occurrence. 'I can't think why else you'd leave me so much money.'

'What aspect of money and payment would you like to discuss first?' he offered, so certain of moral victory he opened his arms in a gesture of encouragement.

To see Razi so cut off from human feeling broke her heart. It hadn't even occurred to him that she might be here to see him, or that what she felt for him was deep and everlasting love that asked for nothing in return. But this wasn't about Lucy Tennant or even Razi al Maktabi, it was about a small defenceless child. She were here in Isla de Sinnebar to tell a man who no longer existed that they were going to have a baby together. The fact that something in Razi's history meant he couldn't imagine a woman loving him as she loved him was irrelevant.

The man she knew had gone and in his place was the ruler of Isla de Sinnebar, a warrior sheikh, who probably knew more about mastering a fiery stallion at the head of his troops than love. And now she was desperate to buy time. She might be strong and determined in her mind, but, unlike Razi, she was human and exhausted. Pregnancy had drained her and the enormity of the task ahead of her had begun to tell. 'Would you mind if I freshened up before we talk? All I need is—'

'Five minutes of my time?' he interrupted.

'If you can spare it?'

'I can spare you five minutes—in my office. When you're ready to see me ring the bell and someone will come to escort you. Don't keep me waiting, Lucy.'

And with a swirl of robes he was gone.

He was a king with measureless powers, a king who had sworn to devote himself to a country and its people, but he was also a man and had thought that part of him locked away before Lucy's reappearance.

She was a brief, bright memory, and must remain so, he told himself firmly. He wasn't a ruler under sufferance. He wanted to be King so that he could change things for the better in Isla de Sinnebar.

He wanted the responsibility that came with rebuilding a backward country and would allow nothing to stand in the way of progress or the happiness of his people—and that included Lucy Tennant. If she wanted more money she could have it, but she could not stay. His first action would be to get her out of the building and away from public view. Her mere presence in a country that was still so backward-looking was all it might take for unsettling rumours to start up.

But she had fainted at his feet and he was concerned about her. She didn't appear to be her usual robust self.

There had always been something luminous about Lucy, but now there was a fragility he hadn't noticed before. Perhaps it was just lack of food—or dehydration, the climate change or jet lag—or perhaps the stress of coming to see him. Whatever—he could at least feed her.

His arrival in the kitchens caused quite a stir. He ordered a picnic to be packed immediately. However suspicious he was of Lucy's motives, hospitality was the way in Isla de Sinnebar and that particular tradition insisted he attended to all of her needs before he sent her on her way.

CHAPTER ELEVEN

SITTING by Razi's side in an unmarked army Jeep, Lucy was filled with apprehension. He had dismissed the driver. The vehicle had been waiting for them with its engine running, at the back door of the Maktabi office building with her luggage already loaded in the back. Razi was wearing jeans, desert boots and a plain black top, with the sleeves cut off to accommodate his biceps and a pair of aviators concealing the expression in his astute green eyes. To a casual observer he would pass for any particularly good-looking government agent with an uneasy suspect at his side. 'Are we going to the airport?' she asked, dry-mouthed.

'Soon.'

So, where were they going? Lucy wondered, her anxiety mounting as the Jeep swept away from the kerb. Her great idea lay in ashes. Telling Razi her wonderful news now would be akin to walking into the lion's den and asking if the lion would like relish with his meal. She couldn't do it. Her first priority had to be going home to England where she could consult a lawyer. 'Is there another flight to the UK today?'

'Not as far as I'm aware.'

She craned her neck to read a sign as Razi drove down a slip road onto the highway. 'Where did you say we were going?'

'I didn't.' As you very well know, his quick glance seemed to say. 'We're going into the desert.'

The desert? Her heart was thundering so violently she felt sick. Why couldn't they have talked at the office as Razi had suggested? Because he didn't want anyone to see him with her, Lucy concluded.

But he could have ordered someone to take her to the airport.

And had chosen not to.

Because he wouldn't want any loose ends, she told herself sensibly, trying to calm down. Razi would never ask anyone to do something he believed was his duty; he took care of his own problems.

The highway cut through the desert, and at one time exploring that would have excited her, but the thought of travelling into such dangerous terrain with a man who could only wish she had never existed was a terrifying prospect.

Razi's grim expression did nothing to allay Lucy's fears. They sat in silence while he drove the same way he made love, with focus and a frightening degree of skill. 'I thought you were joking about the desert,' she said nervously as he took a turning off the highway.

'I never joke,' he said grimly.

Not these days. And now there was only the shimmering heat haze in front of them and the wilderness beyond.

When they arrived at their destination he had barely put the brake on before Lucy tumbled out of the Jeep. She gazed around in fear at what he realised must appear nothing more than featureless desert and mountainous dunes to her. 'There's more to come,' he assured her, springing down to stand by her side.

She didn't answer and the tension in her shoulders filled him with the urge to comfort her. He had forgotten how natural and unaffected she was, or that he hadn't met anyone like her before or since. He made the effort to see things through her eyes and then he realised that what was familiar to him was strange and threatening to Lucy, and as she stumbled on the sand he leapt forward to steady her. 'You're trembling,' he said, taking tighter hold of her. 'You've no need to be frightened of me.' He stared into her anxious eyes. 'I come here all the time,' he explained. 'It's quite safe. I thought it would be better for our talk than a sterile office building.'

'It's certainly more discreet,' she observed shrewdly.

He had forgotten how perceptive she was too. 'As soon as we've had our talk,' he promised, 'I'll take you back.'

She looked at him as if to say she knew as well as he did that the time of her departure would depend on him just as her arrival had and that he held all the cards. 'Lead on,' she said, firming her jaw.

Something had changed. Lucy was stronger than when they'd first met...

Whatever it was he didn't have long to find out.

Razi was a master of surprise. He'd sprung the first surprise at the door of his office where he'd been dressed in casual clothes and ready to leave, and now this drive into the wild interior. At first she thought there was nothing to see other than sand, but as Razi led the way up the shallow side of a dune and she saw the panorama on the other side she realised her dreams of a desert kingdom had been insipid stabs at conjuring the reality.

'No comment?' Razi demanded.

She was too stunned to speak. 'It's very beautiful,' she said at last. This was a massive understatement. The brow of the dune was flat, allowing them to stand securely and look over the surrounding land. She was acutely aware of Razi at her side, sharing the moment as she gazed up into a metallic-blue sky streaked lemon and baby pink. There was a gash of neon-orange at the horizon and all the vivid colours of the dying sun were reflected on the surface of a glittering oasis, whose water was so clear she could see each tiny pebble on the sandy floor. Lush green palm trees provided a frame and there was even fruit hanging thickly amongst the fronds. But it was the pavilion on the bank of the oasis, with its ivory silk walls framed in indigo dusk, undulating lazily in the night-time breezes, that really held her attention. 'Is that a traditional structure?'

'It's mine,' he said, following her gaze.

'It's so romantic.' She regretted the words the moment they left her mouth.

Razi remained silent, staring out across his desert kingdom. He moved down the dune and she followed him. He strode to the pavilion where he held the curtain aside for her to enter. As she dipped her head and brushed past him she was aware of his exotic scent, and as she walked deeper into the shaded interior she felt the heat of his stare on her back.

As she looked around he explained, 'Everything you see here was produced in this country.'

It said something about a man who could take his pick from the world's riches, and yet had furnished his desert retreat only with those items that carried a particular significance to him. Razi's devotion to the Isla de Sinnebar couldn't have been more starkly illustrated and she realised his trip to the mountains when they'd met had been one last indulgence before Razi returned to rule—and that her part in that trip had been nothing more than an entertainment for him.

'What do you think?' he said, interrupting these thoughts.

She brushed away the sadness and concentrated on her surroundings. 'I think it's magical,' she said honestly. Everything was new and strange to her—she had everything to learn about his country. As she ran the palm of her hand over the fabric walls Razi explained that they were woven so fine to keep out the sand. So like the furniture they were functional as well as beautiful. It was like a treasure trove—Aladdin's cave, she thought as she turned around to examine everything. There were chests of burnished ebony inlaid with mother of pearl, pierced brass tables and fabulous rugs intricately woven in jewel colours. Plump silk cushions invited rest, while polished lamps cast a subdued and honeyed light. As if a veil had dropped from her eyes, Lucy saw the heritage she was denying her child. The interior of the pavilion was so lovely she yearned for the opportunity to ask Razi for the history of every piece so she could squirrel the information away to tell her baby when the time was right. But how could she do that when he didn't want idle conversation—and when the time would never be right? How could she ever have a normal conversation with him when she was concealing such a vital piece of news?

He offered her water, which she drank, and then she waited while he went back to the Jeep to collect the picnic he'd brought with them. This gave her an opportunity to look at things more closely, and now she noticed the platters of sweetmeats and the jugs of juice. 'You planned this,' she said when he returned.

'You gave me around five minutes, I seem to remember,' he said dryly, placing the basket of food on the ground.

And servants would rush to do his bidding, Lucy realised. Razi had everything in the material sense, and yet he seemed to have lost his joie de vivre, along with his capacity to love or even empathise with a fellow human being. How could that be good for his country? How could a fun-free life with a duty-bound father be good for her child?

'Many of these gifts were left by the Bedouin,' he explained, oblivious to her concerns. 'And my brother uses the place sometimes.'

Lucy shuddered at Razi's mention of the man known as The Sword of Vengeance. 'You two must be very close,' she ventured.

'We trust each other completely.'

What would Ra'id make of her? Lucy wondered. She had to remind herself the great Sheikh probably wouldn't think about staff at all.

Some of this must have shown on her face, she guessed as Razi dipped his head to stare at her. 'Are you unwell?' he demanded.

'I'm fine,' she lied, knowing pregnancy had taken hold of both her body and her turbulent thoughts.

'Here, drink this.' He poured another glass of water.

'I'm perfectly all right,' she insisted as he stared closely at her. But gullible was one thing Razi had never been.

He was instantly suspicious. There had been too much force behind Lucy's assurance that she was all right. So what was she hiding? He refused to consider the most obvious explanation. Lucy was too honest to hide something so vital from him. But her eyes were wary and she was very pale…

The desire to protect Lucy and to defend a country combined in a surge of longing. He couldn't have both and had been right to get her out of the city and away from prying eyes. He could have taken her to any number of places, but had chosen the sultry, seductive setting of the Maktabi Lagoon, a place so rich in ecological treasures he and his brother Ra'id only allowed the passing Bedouin to use it. Why here? Because the desert freed him. This place was his haven when he needed to recall how it had felt to be free. And he supposed that, whatever Lucy's motives for coming to Isla de Sinnebar, some part of him that still remembered the time they had shared in the ski resort had wanted her to see this special place.

And now he wanted her to stay.

Why shouldn't she stay?

He argued violently with himself, only to come up with the answer that rules might be made to be broken, but that was not the type of leader he intended to be. But for now he'd make her comfortable. 'I keep a selection of robes in that chest over there,' he said, viewing her city clothes with some degree of sympathy.

'For your visitors?'

There was the faintest edge to her voice that made him smile inwardly. This was the Lucy he remembered: fire beneath the ice. And jealous too? He let that pass. What else could he do when he had changed her? He had always wanted Lucy to have confidence and self-belief, and now she had. 'The Bedouin leave a selection of robes and other products when they use this trail through the desert,' he explained. 'That's our custom here. If we have more than we need we pass it on to our neighbour—so, please, feel free to choose a robe to wear.' She was hot and flustered in her workplace armour and would be more comfortable in a loose local robe, plus he'd like to see her wearing one—one last image for him to keep. 'There's no one but us around,' he pointed out. 'Why don't you take a dip in the oasis to freshen up and then choose a robe?'

Maybe if she reversed that? Lucy thought as Razi strolled over to the ebony chest. She was still on edge with her mind full of what she had come to tell him. She watched as he raised the lid of a chest and rifled inside before pulling out a shimmering robe. In the palest shade of sky blue, it was embroidered with tiny pearls and diamanté, and was perhaps the most beautiful item of clothing she had ever seen. But as he held it up and the light streamed through it she realised it was completely sheer. 'Don't you have anything a little less revealing?'

'This?' he suggested, pulling out what was clearly a man's robe.

'That's perfect.' She nodded, plucking the dark, home-spun robe out of his hands. It would go round her three times at a guess.

He was cooking over an open fire when Lucy returned from her swim. He'd had plenty of time to think while she'd been enjoying the lagoon, and every answer he'd come up with to explain her unexpected visit remained the same. He shrugged it off, refusing to believe she'd keep something like that from him.

'You're cooking,' she said with surprise.

'I still have to eat when I'm in the desert.' He almost smiled. He hadn't meant to relax, but the desert did that to him. He never felt more calm than when he was alone in this isolated splendour. He had always thought he was ready to see Lucy too—images already formed and complete in his head—but she never failed to surprise him. This time he sprang to his feet to save her embarrassment. The robe she had chosen to wear was trailing round her feet, and instead of winding the headdress, or *howlis*, as it was known in Isla de Sinnebar, around her head and face leaving only her eyes on view, she had draped it over her hair like a scarf. 'Here, let me,' he offered, risking danger just in touching her—and more of the same in being close. Not that he'd ever shrunk from danger, but when that danger came in the form of a woman he wanted to touch—a woman he had always believed to be pure and uncomplicated and now had his doubts about…

'I'm not wearing it right?' she said anxiously.

Taking hold of her water-cooled hands, he moved them away from her head to arrange the yards of fabric. He dragged greedily on her intoxicating wildflower scent while he was covering her face until only her concerned eyes were on view. 'You are now,' he said, relieved that her lips were covered. 'Now all I need is a camera.'

'You're laughing at me.'

'You used to have a sense of humour,' he reminded her, aiming this over his shoulder as he returned to the fire.

'And so did you,' she called after him.

There was a moment of complete stillness between them as if they both accepted this, and then she went inside the pavilion to sort out her clothes, leaving him to see to the food. When she returned he tipped the omelette he had prepared for her onto a palm frond.

'Eat,' he encouraged as she sat cross-legged on the rug in front of the fire. He was still trying to talk himself into believing Lucy's pallor was due to the long flight—or to dehydration—or to not eating for some time—to anything other than what made the most sense.

'This is delicious,' she said with surprise.

They were both off guard and almost exchanged a smile, but Lucy's gaze dropped too quickly. He knew without doubt then that she was hiding something big from him.

She tossed away the headdress and began devouring the omelette as if she hadn't eaten for days. He remembered her appetite for more than food. Here there was privacy afforded by mile upon mile of unseen sand. That she wanted him, he had no doubt. That he wanted Lucy had never been in doubt—and now more than ever. This was one last chance to taste what might have been and her absence from his life had only sharpened his appetite.

She glanced at him as if she could read his thoughts, but there was strain in her eyes—the strain of keeping that secret from him.

CHAPTER TWELVE

WHEN Lucy had finished eating she went to rinse her hands in the oasis. Razi braced himself for her return when he knew he would be hearing something monumental. But she surprised him once again.

'I'd like to talk to you about money,' she said, settling down on the opposite side of the fire.

He scratched his jaw. 'I admire your candour.'

She had to make this work. There was no point wishing she and Razi could thrill together at the news of their child, when Razi was the ruler of a country and she was a chef. The best she could hope for was that she could get a good job back in England and secure her baby's future. Meanwhile, she had to open a discussion that would allow her to go home. 'I realised there could only be one reason why you left me so much money—'

'You did?' Razi's green eyes glinted.

'You wanted me to open a restaurant.' She let this hang, daring him to disagree. If he did, it would turn their brief, though precious—at least to her—liaison into something sordid.

'That was my intention,' he confirmed.

This gave Lucy the courage to make her next suggestion. It was bold, but it was a way of keeping in touch with Razi, so that when she was ready to tell him about their child they could discuss their baby's progress—though only over a boardroom table; something she believed he might agree to and she could handle. It was better than the prospect of never seeing him again and infinitely better than entrusting their child to strangers to pass between them. 'I have identified a small site suitable for a restaurant and I've drawn up a business plan—'

'Do you have it with you?'

'Well, no…' The one—the only thing on her mind when she had left England for Isla de Sinnebar had been the future of her child. She pressed on. 'I'd like to use some of your money to help me with the start-up.'

'And that's why you're here?'

It went against the grain to tell him even the smallest white lie, but when the stakes were so high and he had just given her a way out… 'If you're interested in taking a look at my predictions I'll email a copy of my proposal to you as soon as I return.'

'I don't believe you didn't think to bring a copy with you,' he told her flatly.

'I didn't presume to—' She dried up. What? She didn't presume to stand her ground in front of the desert king? Razi knew her better than that. And while she hesitated it only took the slightest adjustment in his gaze to call her a liar. She couldn't appear strong in one area and then fall back on the old, self-effacing Lucy when it suited her. 'At first, all I wanted to do was return the money,' she admitted, remembering how humiliated and angry she'd felt when she first found the pile of banknotes on the nightstand.

'And now your situation has changed?'

'I got an idea for a restaurant.' She couldn't hold his gaze and her cheeks were blazing.

Razi's expression darkened. 'So you want to open a restaurant and you've drawn up a plan?' Springing to his feet, he stood towering above her, his anger palpable. 'You didn't have to come to Isla de Sinnebar to tell me that, Lucy. You could have emailed me your proposals as you've just offered to do now. You're a hopeless liar,' he said grimly. 'Isn't it about time you told me the truth?'

The ease that had briefly existed between them had vanished and in its place tension snapped like an oncoming storm. She stood up to face him. 'You're right. I'm sorry I came—I should have realised—'

'Realised what, Lucy?'

There was something potent in Razi's stillness that made her body yearn and fear him all at the same time, but she should have remembered that he moved a lot faster than she did. She should have remembered what it felt like to have him hold her firmly in place in front of him so she was drowning in his potent heat.

'You should have realised what, Lucy?' Razi pressed fiercely. 'That I'm not going to be easily drawn in—or fobbed off? What should you have realised? Why are you here?'

'Let me go—'

'Not until you tell me the real reason for your surprise visit. After—what is it? Almost twelve weeks?'

'You make it sound so—'

'Suspicious?' Razi rapped, all semblance of civilised behaviour stripped from his face. 'How would you feel in my place? Suspicious would just be a start, I'm guessing—'

'Please let me go.'

'Not until you tell me the truth—'

'I can't…'

'Why not?'

Her voice might be broken, but from some primal depth the fire of being a new mother rushed out of her in a shout. 'I just can't! Okay?'

'Don't ask me to believe you've come halfway round the world on the off chance I'd be free to speak to you about some plan you have to open a restaurant. Even if you didn't email those plans through first, you'd make an appointment—'

'I tried to.'

Razi called every bluff she'd had and had never seemed more the desert King than he did in that moment. He was so darkly forbidding, she was shivering with fright, but that was no use to her here. She had to think of her baby and for the sake of that child she would fight. She wasn't ashamed of herself or her baby and Razi was right on all counts. If she had wanted to put a business proposition in front of him a face-to-face meeting would have been unnecessary at this stage. Only a child would bring her here to face him. And now that child's father was waiting for her to prove herself unworthy of being a mother. She had to tell him.

'Are you pregnant?' Razi demanded, stealing the initiative.

His instinct shocked her to the point where she couldn't speak for a moment. 'Yes, I'm pregnant.' She would never deny the existence of her child.

'You're pregnant?' Razi's voice had taken on a new and frightening tone as if he had hit her with the most extreme reason he could think of for her coming to Isla de Sinnebar and had only just realised it might be true.

Lucy's hands flew to protect her womb as Razi stared at her and for one glittering moment the prospect of having

Razi al Maktabi as her protector and the hands-on father of her child was a heady prospect, but then she accepted reality. He would never acknowledge a foreigner who was virtually a member of his kitchen staff as an equal and a royal child would never be allowed to leave the country. She had told him the truth and was damned. If she hadn't told him she would have been equally damned, for then she would never have been able to look her child in the eyes and tell that child the truth about her father.

'So that's why you fell into a faint at my feet—and why you looked so pale when we arrived in the desert.' Razi's expression darkened. 'Have you no sense of responsibility? No concern for anyone but yourself? Don't you care about your child? Or—'

'You?' Lucy interrupted. She had paled beneath Razi's onslaught, but rallied to defend the truth. 'I care about you more than you know.'

Even as he exclaimed with disbelief she saw a look in his eyes she'd never seen before. It spoke of a fierce pain— a pain from the past that still had the power to hurt him. 'I'm pregnant, Razi,' she said quietly, 'and that's a fact as well as a cause for rejoicing. I'm afraid you'll just have to get used to it—I have.'

Get used to it? He was already changing. A baby? He was ice. He was fire. He didn't dare to hope. 'A baby or *our* baby?' he demanded, fuelled by unbearable suspicion.

'*My* baby.'

'That doesn't answer my question, Lucy,' he told her coldly. But he could tell it was a baby she had loved from the first moment she had realised she was pregnant. He didn't question Lucy's maternal instinct. She would defend her child to her last breath. He envied her that depth of feeling. But all Lucy's thoughts were centred on the baby and on her duties as that baby's mother and this passionate new love had blinded her to reality and to the world outside her own cosmos. She could have no idea of the repercussions inside a country like Isla de Sinnebar if the news leaked out. 'How do you know it's our child?' he said, feeling calmer now his mind had cleared to make way for this most crucial of tests.

'Because there hasn't been anyone else,' she said, appearing more vulnerable than ever as she made this innocent admission.

He closed his heart to her. 'How do I know that? How do I know I can trust you?'

Her steady gaze shamed him, but still he drove on to seek the truth. 'How do I know that I'm not one of many guests you…entertained?'

He stopped the flat of her hand before it reached his face, holding her wrist in a non-negotiable grip.

'Let go of me!' she insisted, struggling to break free.

His answer was to bring her closer so he could stare into her wounded eyes. 'I'll release you when you calm down and tell me the truth—and I mean all of it.'

This wasn't the civilised man she had met in Val d'Isere, but a warrior king, who was burning up inside with pain and fury. 'Let go of me. Of course it's our baby. I've never been with anyone else. If you need proof we can have a DNA test once the baby is born.'

Razi held on to her, his gaze unwavering.

'Do you really think I would fly halfway round the world,' Lucy demanded, throwing Razi's taunt back at him, 'without knowing it was your baby? I don't lie.'

She stared down at his hands on her arms and he

released her. 'I also have a bank statement, showing that I set up an account exclusively for the money you left at the chalet, and that I never touched a penny of it.'

'So you put your plans for a restaurant first, your child second and telling me about our baby a very poor third?' He threw up his hands in disbelief.

'I'm not saying that.' This was all going horribly wrong. She had never meant to lie to him.

'When, Lucy? When did you intend to tell me?'

'When I returned to England,' she confessed steadily. 'I came here thinking you were Mac—a businessman—only to discover you were the ruling Sheikh—'

And a man who clearly mistrusted women, believing them incapable of love. Lucy only had to look into Razi's eyes to know that his inner scars went a lot deeper than she had previously supposed. Some long-held wound was festering inside him. She couldn't know the details, but she could feel the effect, and while part of her was filled with compassion for his pain, the part of her that was a mother— and that part was swiftly becoming all of her—was terrified at the thought that the ruling Sheikh of Isla de Sinnebar's only interest now was to secure custody of their child.

And what power did she have to stop him? Once Razi had done that she'd be his captive for life, for she would never abandon her child to the care of strangers. Razi lived on an island halfway across the world from where she lived. How would that work? When would she see her baby? How could she bear her child to live so far away from her? She couldn't. And Razi wouldn't want her here.

It was a problem to which there was no solution, and in this case the only form of attack was defence. 'Why did you bring me to the desert? To show me a valuable ecological site? I don't think so, Razi. You brought me here to get me away from the city and prying eyes. You brought me here because you're ashamed of me.'

'I'm not ashamed of you,' he insisted. 'Why did you come to the Isla de Sinnebar if not to trap me in some way?'

'What? That's absurd. How would I do that when you're an all-powerful king?'

'That's what I want to find out.' He raked his thick black hair with angry fingers. 'Has it occurred to you that a scandal like this could rock my country? No—I didn't think so. If I acknowledge this child it will be seen as my first act in power. How will that look to my people? And the mother of that child a foreigner in this, the most traditional of countries.'

He made her feel as if she had done something wrong— and there was no mention of a baby to love, just a country to be ruled with a rod of iron, heartlessly, like a company meeting targets to be approved by the ruling Sheikh. 'It seems to me you support all the antiquated beliefs you have sworn to eradicate. And as for me—I don't want anything from you.'

'Well, that's clearly untrue,' Razi informed her coldly, 'or you wouldn't be here.'

'I thought you should know, that's all. I'm not trying to trap you into anything. I'm quite capable of standing on my own feet without your help.'

'So you plan to have the child and I have no say in the matter?'

'That's not it at all—'

'It must be one or the other,' Razi insisted coldly. 'Which is it, Lucy? Blackmail? Or sob story?'

CHAPTER THIRTEEN

LUCY drew on her inner strength. 'The man I knew in Val d'Isere would never have said that. And let me tell you something else,' she added without giving Razi chance to speak. 'You say you care about a country. I don't believe you. How can you care about anything if you're incapable of love? And if you're incapable of love, I don't want you to have anything to do with my child—'

'Our child,' he reminded her fiercely. 'Or so you say—'

'Yes, I do say,' Lucy insisted, bracing for battle. Where her child was concerned she was fearless.

He had never felt such wild emotions. He wanted to hug Lucy and rejoice—yet also turn his back on her and never see her again. He rued the day he'd met her and yet longed for her to stay. She had to stay if she was having his child. The realisation that he was about to become a father had left him drowning in happiness, while the thought that anyone, even Lucy, might imagine she could keep him from that child was an abomination he refused to consider. The memory of a child living in lonely isolation, waiting for his brother's visits to break the monotony of being cared for by strangers, was still too raw for that. If she was having his child he would not be denied the joy of seeing that child grow up. The thought of anyone but him protecting the baby, loving it as he would, was unthinkable. He wouldn't stand on the sidelines for Lucy—for anyone.

'Will I embarrass your wife?'

'My wife?' The red mist of anger was still on him as he refocused dazedly.

'I presume there's got to be a wife soon,' she said, turning from shy supplicant to virago in a moment. 'Tell me,' she insisted. 'I have to know. I have to protect my child. I don't imagine you'd want me here in Isla de Sinnebar muddying the water when the time comes for you to choose a wife—'

'There is no wife,' he roared, stopping her, 'or ever likely to be a wife.' The face of his cousin Leila flashed into his mind. He had sent her back to university where she so dearly wanted to be and then had dispatched her greedy father with a flea in his ear and a cheque large enough to keep him off Leila's back.

'So, you're married to duty?' Lucy suggested, taking another tack.

'And what if I am?'

'That isn't what I want for my baby, Razi. And if you're closed off from love what good are you to a country?'

'Let me be the judge of that,' he snapped. 'I'm interested in cold, hard fact—like what do you want for your child, Lucy?' He was already calculating the amount.

Her wounded gaze said no child of hers could ever be bought. 'I want my baby to be loved,' she said quietly.

'Yet you think me incapable of love?'

She didn't answer. She didn't need to and as his own doubts kicked in he turned on the person least deserving of his anger. 'You should have told me the moment you knew you were pregnant. We could have arranged something.'

'Like what?' she exclaimed fearfully, lifting her arm almost as if she was shielding her face from so much pain. 'Don't say any more, Razi,' she begged him. 'Don't say things I know you don't mean.'

He took himself aside until he was calmer. 'I mean I would have supported you and the baby,' he said then.

'If I were discreet? If I bowed my head—hid my child?'

'Did you really think this was something you could keep from me?'

'It's why I'm here.'

'And you think I'd be happy to have no say in my child's life? How little you know me.'

How true, Lucy thought. They had shared the ultimate intimacy, but they were still two strangers facing up to one of life's major turning points together. They had everything to learn about each other—everything to learn about how they would go on from here. But they had to go on from here and she had to make Razi listen. 'I wasn't keeping anything from you. I waited for three months to be as sure as I could be that the pregnancy was safe.'

His reaction shocked her. Wheeling away, Razi put his head in his hands as if for once there was a problem he couldn't solve. She gave him space, sensing the renewed onslaught of his pain, though in some ways it was a relief to see such a passionate response from a man who had grown so cold.

Razi was a warrior, exotic, fierce and passionate— while she was a chef, neat and tidy—cautious, some might say; at least, she had been cautious up to meeting Razi. They both had so much to offer their child if only they could put their differences behind them. They must do that because only then could they start to build a future for their baby. But right now Razi was at his most untouchable, his most remote, with every sinew and muscle in his body stretched tight.

There had never been a moment when she had been frightened of Razi, but she was frightened now, yet this was the very moment when she must reach out to him, while the pull of duty was warring with his warmer, human side. For all her ignorance of such weighty problems, one thing she did know—a country run for the sake of duty would be a cold and barren place. She touched his arm, expecting him to send her away—or, worse, ignore her. She was used to being invisible, but that didn't mean she liked it. You never got used to that sort of thing. It always hurt. She stood quietly, feeling foolish as the silence dragged on, but then the miracle she'd hoped for happened. Razi turned to stare at her. He didn't speak, but the fact that he had responded at all was enough for now.

There was a world of questions in Lucy's eyes, any one of which he could pick and break her heart. 'I have decided that this is the way forward,' he said instead, planning his words carefully.

He had no reason to mistrust Lucy, not if he made himself remember her innocence at the chalet. So he was already considering the timing for acknowledging Lucy's baby in public. He would sell the concept of an unmarried ruling Sheikh who already had a child to the older tribesman as proof of his fertility, turning disapproval into approval at a stroke. Yes, he was a cynic; business had made him that way. Before accepting the Phoenix throne he had founded an empire largely on his wits. For sure there had been no help from his father, the ruling Sheikh. Plus, he had vowed to revise the antiquated laws of Isla de Sinnebar, bringing them into line with the modern world—so this *would* be his first act and he would turn it into a positive act.

He would stop at nothing to make a better job of parenting than his own absentee parents, but he wanted the throne too—and not for selfish reasons, but because he knew he could bring progress and benefits to his people. With good management and careful husbandry of the land and indigenous species, Isla de Sinnebar would thrive. There would be justice for all, a first-class healthcare system and the best education his money could buy. This was both his goal and his passion. He existed for no other purpose than to serve Isla de Sinnebar. He had not bargained for the additional blessing of a child, but as he outlined his plans for Lucy he realised it wasn't a question of wanting to take the child from her, but more a matter of security for both Lucy and their baby. He expected her to fight him when she heard his proposals. He expected her to feel disappointed that she couldn't be anything more to him than the mother of his child, but he was confident she could only be reassured when he told her what he meant to do to secure her future.

Lucy listened as Razi spelled out her glittering new life. The biggest surprise of all was his intention to acknowledge their child. She was so stunned she didn't hear everything he was saying and had to ask him to repeat things.

Her eyes widened with disbelief. She hadn't come to Isla de Sinnebar for this. She was to have a wonderful home of her own choosing in England—a country estate with stables, if she liked. She would have an income appropriate for the mother of a royal child, and a private jet at her disposal so she could visit their child—within reason—whenever she wanted to. There was no mention of joint parenting—joint anything. It was a clean cut. It was a life according to the old saying—beyond the dreams of avarice—but greed she had none, just a longing for the family life she had always dreamed of, where children would thrive and grow in the full knowledge that they were loved. 'You're very generous,' she said politely when Razi had finished laying out all the benefits that would accrue from being, not even a royal mistress, but a royal brood mare.

He made a casual gesture, as if paying a king's ransom to keep her out of sight was more than worth it.

She couldn't leave it here. She had to find a way to touch him. 'And you, Razi—what part do you intend to play in our baby's life?'

He looked at her as if she were mad. 'A full part, of course.'

'And you'll have time for that? You'll have time to be a full-time parent?'

He waved his hand dismissively. 'You don't understand the life I lead.'

'Clearly.'

'I have over a thousand staff working for me in Isla de Sinnebar alone.'

'Staff,' she said quietly. 'Is that how you were brought up, Razi? By staff?'

She could not have predicted the look in his eyes. She could never have guessed they would fill with pain. She knew immediately the cause of Razi's seething anger and her heart went out to him, but where her own child was concerned it did not soften her by one iota. Her baby was not going to suffer the same fate as its father—and if that meant there would have to be some big changes in her own life, so be it. 'I'm going to stay,' she said.

Razi could not have looked more shocked. 'You can't stay,' he argued.

'Of course I'll stay,' she insisted. 'And I don't need a big house—just somewhere safe where I can bring up my child happily. You can visit any time you like. I would never keep you from your baby, Razi, just as I would never expect you to deny me access to my child.'

He stared at her in silence. Was that because he couldn't believe what she was offering? Lucy guessed she was very different from Razi's mother. He might not have spelled out the details of his childhood—he didn't have to: it was all there on his face. His mother had been compliant, she guessed, and most probably petted and pampered for falling into line. But then the old Sheikh had tired of her and she had been ignored.

Well, Lucy Tennant was prepared to do none of this. She would make her own way in life. 'I'm offering to stay without condition or expectation,' she explained when Razi remained silent. 'With your permission, I imagine I'll be allowed to open a restaurant.'

'What?' he cut across her.

'A restaurant,' she said patiently. 'It seems the obvious thing.'

'To you, maybe, but I cannot allow you to work.'

Lucy frowned. At a stroke Razi had forbidden her to have a career.

She must be reasonable, she warned herself. She could see that maybe she'd made a blunder—fronting a restaurant would be too high profile. 'I could be a silent partner—I could run things from the kitchen without ever showing my face. We have to find a solution, Razi. We must. We have to make this work.'

As he stared at her he realised that before this moment he hadn't believed a woman capable of a selfless act, but

Lucy had proved him wrong. She had proved herself in so many ways even he didn't think it was fair she had to continue doing so. It seemed some people were always fighting with their backs against the wall, while others had it handed to them on a plate. With Ra'id's help he had fought his way up and there was nothing lacking in his life, while Lucy was completely at his mercy.

She stood facing him, expecting nothing, asking nothing. He touched her cheek almost reverently, growing increasingly aware of her sacred role. 'I'll make sure you're well taken care of.'

By whom? her steady gaze asked him.

'Surely you can see the sense in my proposals?' he demanded, tightening his grip on her arms.

He had not expected her eyes to fill with tears, but having all the strength and every advantage he let her go. 'Don't look so downcast. I'll buy you two homes—one here and one in England, but you can't work. It wouldn't be—'

'Appropriate?' she supplied softly. 'I haven't come here looking for handouts, Razi. I don't want anything from you in the material sense. All I ask is your promise never to part me from our child.'

'And to change centuries of tradition?'

'If women don't work here, don't you think you're wasting a valuable resource? If traditions have been in place for centuries, maybe they're due an update. Sorry,' she said, seeing his face tense. 'It's really none of my business.'

As he stared at her he found himself wishing that it were her business.

CHAPTER FOURTEEN

RAZI shook his head in despair. At Lucy's naivety at thinking he could change centuries of tradition? She only wished she could tell him everything in her heart: how she loved him, how she wanted him—and not for his power or for his wealth, or even his good looks, or for any of the other obvious advantages a man as deeply layered and endlessly fascinating as Razi possessed, but for the simple pleasure of being in his company. She couldn't conceive of a palace grand enough or jewels big enough to compete with a glance from him when that glance was full of warmth and connection between them.

'What if I promise never to part you from your child?' he said. 'Is that enough?'

'It's all I've ever wanted.'

'In that you are unique,' he admitted, his lips tugging with just the faintest show of the old humour.

It might be all she'd ever wanted, but it wasn't everything. She wanted Razi's love too, but that was a fantasy too far. She settled for, 'I promise I won't embarrass you, Razi. I'll live a quiet life out of the public eye. I'm not missing anything. I've always been a backroom girl with no idea about fashion or moving in society—'

He cut her off with a laugh that sounded achingly like Mac's.

'What's so funny?' She knew deep down inside. She would never be exposed to society, or have any need to learn about fashion; the life she had planned out—the future they had practically agreed on—included none of that. She would live somewhere in the country where he could visit discreetly.

She gasped as Razi cupped her chin and made her look at him. 'I'm laughing because you're funny,' he said, his glance slipping from her eyes to her lips. 'Your ideas are funny. Your notion of how I live and what's important to me is so far off the mark, it's funny.'

'I'm sorry.'

'Don't be.'

A world of possibilities opened up as Razi's thumb caressed her jaw. She could do this… She could do just about anything to be with him…

Razi's smile was slow, and confident enough to make her believe anything was possible. Her breath sounded ragged in the silence as she waited, suspended somewhere between hoping things were changing and knowing deep down they could never change enough to make all of her dreams come true.

She was right. The tension between them subsided and he let her go. His next words proved that while she had been desperate to believe in a fantasy Razi's quick mind had covered all the bases. Every conceivable facility would be made ready for the expectant mother of the royal child. Lucy and her baby would want for nothing. Name it, and she could have it. If she preferred a different consultant—a different nursing team—anything—everything—too much of everything—was hers for the asking, while the one thing she wanted and longed for so badly, which was a normal family life, could never be hers. But as her emotions welled, so did her longing for Razi—one more night of pretending they could be together and she could cope with anything. One night of love to last a lifetime didn't seem so greedy. One more night of knowing how it felt to be loved…

With his senses so keenly tuned to Lucy he knew almost before she did when she surrendered her ideas to his. He was still coming to terms with the miracle of new life and the fact that Lucy was carrying his child and felt a great sense of wonder. There was also the urge to stake his claim again.

'This is crazy,' she murmured, shivering with desire as his lips brushed her mouth.

'That's the weakest protest I ever heard,' he observed, slowly backing her towards the entrance to the pavilion.

'I must be crazy,' she protested, reaching up to rest her hands on his shoulders.

'A little crazy goes a long way with me,' he murmured, giving her waist a reassuring squeeze.

Razi lowered her onto cushions that supported her frame and yet moulded themselves to her body in the most comfortable way. The curtain over the entrance was still drawn back to allow streamers of moonlight to decorate their cushioned bed. The interior of the pavilion was shaded and lit by two brass oil lamps and an incense burner. She was surrounded in a haze of delicious scent and refreshing night-time breezes kept her cool, but even in Razi's arms she was restless. There was so much to be decided yet and maybe this was a mistake. 'This is wrong.'

'Wrong?' Razi murmured against her mouth. Removing

her ugly robe, he tossed it aside. 'There's nothing wrong with this,' he said, shooting a wicked glance down the length of her body.

Just one more night...

It was as if all the humour and worldliness that had once drawn her to him was back. There were no divisions between them now, just the gasping, pleading sounds she was making as Razi rubbed his thumb across her bottom lip. Taking her face in his hands, he kissed her slowly, deeply, until her anxiety subsided and all thoughts of tomorrow disappeared.

'I'm almost frightened to touch you now you're carrying my child,' he murmured, kissing the tender place on her neck and then her collarbone, before travelling down to tug and tease her painfully engorged nipples, before moving on to lave her belly with his tongue. 'Almost,' he added in a wry murmur when she groaned in complaint. He proved this by working his magic on her swollen lips with delicate raids of his tongue. 'You taste different—fuller, richer, sweeter...'

And she was almost frantic with desire. How she longed to be full of him, stretched by him...loved by him. Where she had hungered for sensation, Lucy realised, now what she hungered for was closeness, reassurance and love.

Springing to his feet, Razi kicked off his boots and unfastened his jeans and as he eased them over his lean hips she realised she had forgotten how beautiful he was—how magnificent. And when he tugged his top over his head, exposing his naked, hard-muscled torso with the rampant lion tattooed in black ink whorls on hard bronze flesh, she wondered if ever a man had been born who was quite so perfect...perfect for her.

She reached for him as he lay beside her, caressing his

face, loving the sharp black stubble that could bring her so much pleasure and so much pain, and dropping kisses on his mouth as his erection, huge and hard, pulsed impatiently against her thighs.

'Slowly, carefully,' he murmured, moving on top of her.

How to tell him that pregnancy had made her hungrier for him than ever and that thanks to the riot of hormones in her body every nerve ending seemed to have received a super-charge of sensation and appetite? Or that some basic need—the need to claim her mate, perhaps—had made her leave her inhibitions at the door? That, together with her need for reassurance, meant there wasn't a moment to lose—she didn't want him carefully and slowly; she wanted him fiercely and now.

She should have remembered Razi's self-control. She might want to remember Razi's resolve and self-control in all future dealings with him, was her last thought before he made all rational thought impossible.

He claimed her slowly and carefully, resisting Lucy's best efforts to urge him on. This was different—she was different, she felt different, just as she had tasted different. Her body was ripe, unique, welcoming, adding both to his desire and to his sense of privilege. He felt possessive too, and with so much sensation going on, his mind went into freefall. He reined back, wanting to please her. Pleasing Lucy was his only goal. She was carrying his child and this was his way of saying thank you.

She had never felt closer to another human being than she felt to Razi that night as they lay, limbs entwined, in the middle of the night. Would they ever get enough of each other? It seemed unlikely. So what was she saying? What was he saying? Would she stay on in Isla de Sinnebar as his mistress and the mother of his child? Could Razi accept her terms? Did she have any right to state them? Her wish to live simply and out of the public eye—was that even possible here? Knowing Razi's intention to run his country like a business beyond blame, would the world's media seize on the new ruler's peccadillo and flaunt their child, leading to endless problems for her baby in the future?

Leaning on her elbow, Lucy fretted as she watched Razi sleeping. If only this were a fantasy she could make every part of it right. He was sprawled on his back with his long, muscular limbs taking up every inch of available space. He looked so beautiful and so peaceful… She traced the line of his lips with her fingertip, pulling her hand away when he turned his head slightly. Now she could see the sweep of jet-black eyelashes casting a blue-black shadow on his sculpted cheeks, and eyebrows that swept upwards like a fiery tartar, or a pirate king…

Razi was a stunning-looking man, but she could never forget he was a king. She traced the tattoo, the symbol of his country, which he had chosen to have indelibly inscribed over his heart. Was there room left in that heart for anyone, woman or child? A shiver gripped her as she thought about it and all her contentment flew away. Razi wasn't just a man she had fallen deeply in love with, he was the ruler of a country. And she was a cook—shortly to become the mother of his child, and, though she might fight with everything in her for her child's right to live free from any taint of shame she could bring it, could any royal child be truly free? Privilege was a poor return for freedom, at least in Lucy's value structure.

Now there was no hope of sleeping. Settling back on the cushions, she turned one last time to drink him in. 'I love you.' How she wished there were more meaningful words to express her feelings for Razi. 'I adore you,' she whispered, and even that didn't come close.

He stirred in his sleep, and, realising her restlessness was disturbing him, Lucy gently disentangled herself and crept silently away.

He stirred and realised Lucy was gone. He was on his feet in an instant, instinct telling him she was swimming in the lagoon, and while swimming at dusk with him when there was light was one thing, swimming in the dead of night when a cloud might cover the moon and she could misjudge the depth—

The thought that anything could happen propelled him out of the pavilion with one thing on his mind: Lucy—to hold her safely in his arms; to make love to her.

The water was like iced silk on her burning skin, and it was sweet and clear. There was firm sand beneath her feet as she plunged deep, loving the sensation of cold against her heated body. She barely had chance to clear her head with a single, lazy lap before she realised she wasn't alone and that Razi was swimming powerfully towards her. Slicing through the water, it took him no time to secure her in his grasp.

The breath left her chest in a rush as he dragged her close. 'What do you think you're doing?' he demanded, his dark eyes flashing fire.

'I'm a strong swimmer, Razi.'

His grip tightened. 'In the pitch-black middle of the night? Alone?' His voice was fierce with concern.

'You said it was safe,' she protested.

'Not on your own. Not again. Not ever. Do you understand me?' He held her back to stare into her face, and then, without waiting for her answer, he secured her in an iron grip and swam for shore.

Or she imagined that was his purpose, but as soon as he was within his depth Razi stood, and in the same fluid movement he took her.

He sank deep, the size of him making her gasp with surprise. She would never become used to him. The darkly exotic light of passion smouldering in his eyes said he understood her need and that this was all for her. Her arousal was extreme. The heat of their bodies and their passion contrasted strongly with the cold of the water to make every sensation bigger, stronger and far more intense. Razi encouraged her to lie back on the cooling water where she could gaze up at a desert moon planted in a field of stars. Could heaven improve on this? she wondered. The majesty of the desert had unleashed the untamed spirit in her heart, Lucy realised, sobbing with pleasure as Razi moved steadily and with absolute intent. He understood her as no one ever had, not just sexually, but in every way. And in turn, she loved his exciting, exotic country, with its passionate people, and its wild, unknowable desert… She loved him.

'I hope I have your full attention?' he murmured, lifting her into his arms so he could add something wicked in his own language.

'Can you doubt it?'

His lips curved.

Her answer to that could only be a groan of deep satisfaction as he sank deep inside again. She hardly had to cling to him at all with the water supporting her and Razi's strong hands controlling her buttocks. He thrust into her just the way she liked while her limbs floated lazily. All the pleasure centred at her core, just as he had intended until finally she couldn't hold him off any longer and her cries of release mingled with those of the eagle owl as it swooped down from its roost to hunt.

'More…' Razi spoke for her, as she was still beyond speech. He kept up a steady beat, gently and persuasively, so that one starburst sensation had barely faded before it began to build into the next. He took her slowly and carefully, making sure she savoured every moment. How could she not? Making love beneath a lemon moon and a deep blue velvet sky filled with diamond pinpoints of light was almost too beautiful, too perfect.

So perfect it frightened her. If only she could capture this experience somehow and bring it out when she was alone to convince herself this had really happened…

'Lucy?' Razi murmured, teasing her with a pass of his roughened cheek against her neck.

'Yes,' she whispered, closing her mind to doubt as he settled her back on the rippling water. She held her breath, waiting for words of reassurance that never came, but Razi knew her body so well—too well, and she had nothing more to do now than rock gently on a pool turned silver beneath the moonlight as he pleasured her, while all the worrying thoughts about the future drifted away.

He watched Lucy come apart in his arms again and again, wondering if she would ever tire, for he was sure he wouldn't. Moonlight had transformed her into an exquisite water nymph, and one whose appetite for sex continued to amaze him. They shared a fierce passion, he reflected as he swung her into his arms to carry her back to the bank, but tonight there was no urgency. They had every hour before dawn to indulge themselves in pleasure before reality reared its ugly head and put a stop to it. Until then he would make this a night to remember for both of them.

When they got back inside the pavilion he swaddled her in towels and dried her tenderly, rejoicing in her beauty as well as in the fact that she would soon be the mother of their child. Lowering her gently onto the silken-cushioned bed, he murmured, 'Hussy,' as she reached for him.

'Your hussy,' she said, smiling while her hand insisted on creating its own sort of havoc.

He drew in a sharp breath as she moved down the bed and then she snatched his breath away, cupping him firmly, her lips brushing him, her tongue teasing him. At first she was a little tentative, as if this was a first for her. He found he was fiercely grateful for that, and had to ask himself just how deeply he was committed to a girl he had so recently thought of keeping out of the public eye before making sure she caught the next flight home. They were way past that, he concluded as Lucy grew bolder. As she laved him with her tongue and closed her lips around him to draw him deeper into her mouth he wondered if he could ever bear to let her go. 'Stop,' he managed huskily, realising how selfish he was being—on all counts.

'Why?' she said, resting her chin on his thigh. 'Are you frightened you might lose control?'

He laughed and lifted her into his arms. She made him laugh. She made him happy. He was wary of losing his heart for the first time in his life. He was frightened of hurting her. She had never put her female powers to the test in quite the same way before and, having done so, she was flying high. She looked triumphant, and more beautiful than ever. She was more flushed, more aroused—more womanly and yet more vulnerable in every way. The newfound confidence on Lucy's face was everything he'd ever wanted to see, and he didn't want anyone to change that—especially not him. 'You're full of surprises.'

'Did I do something wrong?' she demanded softly as he swung her beneath him.

'You did everything right,' he reassured her. 'So right I had to make you stop.'

Her eyes reflected her innocence and her desire to please—to please him. He would never abuse that. It brought out all his protective instincts. 'I won't do anything that puts your pleasure at risk.'

A shadow crossed her eyes and he knew what she was thinking. This was about more than pleasure and in the morning they would have to face that. Where would they go from here? What did the future hold for Lucy—for her baby—for their child? 'It will be all right,' he promised. The clock was already ticking, but he refused to hear it—not yet.

'How long do we have?' she whispered as if she knew everything he was thinking.

'Time enough.' Teasing her lips apart with lazy passes of his tongue, he nudged his way between her legs, thrusting deep, exulting as Lucy's eager body moved to claim him. Whatever the future held, one thing was sure; few people were lucky enough to ever know a night like this.

CHAPTER FIFTEEN

THEY enjoyed a feast in the middle of a balmy night—fresh fruit, which Razi had brought in the picnic hamper, along with hunks of delicious local bread and creamy cheese—before making love again. It was in the sleepy, contented aftermath, when Lucy was nestled safe in Razi's arms, that he surprised her by confiding something of his childhood. The thought that she had touched him enough for that, and that trust was slowly building between them, was like a tiny flame she wanted to shield with her hands to help it to grow. When he told her about his mother she felt fiercely moved that he would do so, as well as fiercely protective of Razi. She was not just protective of her baby now, but of the man she loved.

His mother's name was Helena, Razi said, naming her for the first time since her death. Helena had been very young and frightened, and had found herself fighting for position in a land where she didn't speak the language, or have any rights to speak of. She had no place to run to, and no one to support her cause, as everyone lived in fear of Razi's father, the ruling Sheikh. She had no money, no contacts to help her to return home, and her sole purpose in life had shrunk to remaining beautiful and available twenty four seven in case his father paid a visit. And for a time, that was enough…

Enough? How could it ever be enough? Lucy wondered, tears stinging her eyes as she thought of the little boy who had never known his mother, other than from cruel gossip amongst the palace servants. She cried too for fear that history might repeat itself.

'Hey,' Razi said, kissing tears from her cheeks, 'I can't keep up with the downpour—and anyway, I've talked enough. It's time for you to tell me your story.'

It was so like him to make light of his history. Razi came with a self-pity delete key. But if anyone had a right to be angry about their parents, it was him. They had never had a chance like this to get to know each other, Lucy realised, and maybe they never would again. Thanks to Razi confiding in her, she understood the father of her child a lot better now, but she was still eager to learn more. 'I'm only interested in you,' she protested.

'Nice try,' he said, 'but I'm still waiting.'

'Nothing I've experienced comes close to a child being shunned by its mother.'

'Let me be the judge of that.'

'Do I take that as an instruction?' She stared into his eyes.

'No.' Razi's smile was slow and sexy. 'That was a command.'

It was always the same, he realised. Lucy never wanted to talk about herself. She had no idea how much she gave away just by adopting that attitude. When she finally gave in enough to share a few anecdotes with him, she only confirmed what he already knew. Listening to her as she laughed and joked her way through her family history, he realised she had felt as much the cuckoo in the nest as he had, and that sharing what they had tonight had brought them closer than he would ever have believed possible. His focus now was on reassuring her. 'All that's in the past,' he said, 'and you have your future to look forward to.'

'Do I, Razi?'

He wished she wouldn't look so sad. He wanted to make her happy—especially when he thought of the lonely child she'd been and the self-doubting young woman she'd grown into. She hadn't told him that, of course—she didn't need to. Instead, she made every excuse for her family and none for herself. 'You did nothing wrong,' he protested when she insisted that she always managed to let her family down. 'Everyone wants to be loved. Everyone wants to be understood. Everyone wants to be heard, and you deserve all those things, Lucy.'

'My family does love me.' She made a wry face. 'They just don't get me.'

'I get you…' Touching her face, he kissed her again, thinking how lucky he was to have this time with her.

'It's not as if I was abandoned like you.'

'It's not as if you had a brother like Ra'id to look out for you.'

'My brothers would have looked out for me—if they'd stopped arguing long enough.'

'I'm sure they would,' he agreed, stifling the urge to take all of them on at once for letting her down. Their loss, he supposed, hiding his feelings from her.

'I'd like to meet your brother, Ra'id.'

'You will.'

There was silence as she took this in. Under what circumstances? He could feel her wondering. Would he smuggle her into the palace for a private audience? Would he employ her in the kitchens and have Ra'id inspect the staff? 'I'd be proud to introduce you to Ra'id.'

'You would?'

'How can you doubt it?'

Maybe because every idyll had to come to an end and theirs just had. She was already sensing Razi starting to distance himself. It was no coincidence he was moving away from her in every way he could, physically and mentally as light strengthened inside the pavilion. She clung to him as dawn broke and for a while he relented and they lay in silence, staring out at the pearly sky streaked with lavender and jasmine yellow, until they both, without saying a word, broke apart and moved away in separate directions.

'I'll get the coffee on,' he said as she thought about taking one last swim.

'It's light now,' she said when Razi frowned, 'and I promise I'll be careful.'

He stared at her for some time and then he let her go. It was more than an acknowledgement that she would take care in the water. When they looked at each other she was telling him she could do this on her own—all of it, and that he had to know that and accept it.

It was a brave stand, but with dawn came reality, and the reality was Razi was a king and she was no one. She could no more make a stand in his country than she could fly, but he stopped short of pointing this out and humiliating her. As she picked up her robe and slipped it on he drew her to him and kissed her briefly—it felt like one last time; one last kiss. 'That was quite a night,' he said dryly, releasing her.

'Yes, it was…'

The look they shared now spoke of more than sex. They

had confided in each other and grown closer just as now they must live apart. She shrugged, as if she could handle that too. 'Don't worry—I understand,' she said as if she were reassuring him. 'And I'll always treasure the confidences you shared with me.'

She turned and walked away proudly, deeply conscious of the child inside her, and of the love in her heart, both for that child and for the man who had fathered her baby. Razi had given her new confidence, and by opening up his heart to her last night he had changed her for good, because now she knew love—she knew how it felt to trust and to be trusted in return, and even if this wasn't going to end in the traditional happy-ever-after, she believed him when he said he would never part her from her child.

She had to believe.

He had always thought the desert changed him, freed him, but now he realised it was only the space it gave him to examine his thoughts that made the difference. As they drank their last coffee in front of the campfire he realised that with Lucy at his side exchanging solitude for companionship had proved even more productive and that *she* had freed something inside him. He'd let someone else in and he'd never done that before. He glanced at her sideways, admiring her composure. They knew where they stood now. He'd take care of her in every way he could, but they'd live their own lives. A night that had started in heat and passion had changed them both. He cared about her. He always would. Perhaps more than cared—perhaps even loved—but that didn't mean there could be a solution to this. She was carrying his child and that had made him instantly protective, but it wasn't love—it couldn't be; it was…something else. The nervous smiles Lucy was darting at him suggested her thoughts had turned to concern too. If only she could know how much he wanted this. If only he could tell her that a family was all he had ever longed for, but he'd always accepted there was a high price to pay for privilege and that for every night of pleasure the bank of duty would exact its revenge. He just hadn't known how much it would hurt. To block it out he turned to practicalities. 'When was your last scan?'

Lucy paused with the coffee cup halfway to her lips. She was sitting opposite Razi in front of the campfire he had rebuilt. Dressed in jeans and a jumper to fend off the early morning chill, she had been glad of the hot coffee to nurse after her swim. Now she put it down. Razi had brought out his phone, which seemed incongruous in the wilderness, but not half as incongruous as a sheikh taking care of her maternity concerns.

'You do have baby scans in England?' he pressed, shooting her one of his intense looks as he stabbed in some numbers.

'Of course we do.'

'Well? Have you had one yet?'

'I have my first appointment when I get back—on Friday.'

'And this scan is for how many weeks of pregnancy?'

'Twelve.' She blushed.

'Twelve—and do you know if everything is progressing well?'

'I presume it is.'

'You presume?'

Razi's tone was a dash of cold water in the face. She had seen the doctor to confirm her pregnancy and was following the protocol set up in her health authority area to the letter. There was only one reason she could think of for Razi putting pressure on her now. 'I won't know the sex of my baby for sure until around seventeen weeks.' When he found out it was a girl as she both knew and suspected in a crazy, mixed-up, newly pregnant way, would he quickly lose interest?

'I want to know you're both healthy,' Razi pointed out in a stinging response to that thought. 'Please allow me to speed up the process.'

'I know I'm having a baby girl.'

The astute sea-green gaze flicked up. 'Mother's instinct is wonderful, I'm sure, but if you don't mind I'd like a medical professional to check you're both okay.'

Reality was pouring in thick and fast now, and as Razi held her gaze all the history behind that remark was reflected in his eyes, and she realised no woman would ever convince him that anything she said was true until she proved herself—and that included Lucy Tennant.

And was there something wrong with employing a belt and braces approach where the health of her child was concerned? She settled for, 'Thank you.'

Razi raised his hand as the call connected and started talking rapidly in Sinnebalese. 'It's all arranged,' he said. 'We leave from here and go straight to the private clinic in the capital.'

'Our news won't be very private if you accompany me.'

'Of course I'll take you there. Who else is going to take you? You're my responsibility and it's my duty to make sure you have the best of care.'

His duty? She had been transformed by happiness up to that moment. She had seen so many emotions cross Razi's eyes while they had been sitting cross-legged round the fire. His expression had even warmed and softened briefly, but there was none of that now. She had been transformed during the course of a cup of coffee from night-time lover into daytime responsibility and it seemed that with every inch the sun crept above the horizon the distance between them was growing.

'If one of my employees needed medical attention,' he said, 'don't you think I would personally ensure they got it?'

She wanted to put her fingers in her ears and blot that out—that was what she thought. Other than that she didn't know what to think that didn't hurt like hell. And that was mean-minded of her, Lucy concluded as Razi stood up and started kicking sand over their fire. She had heard nothing but praise for staff relations at Maktabi Communications since taking a closer interest in a certain R. Maktabi's business card; she should be glad she was under the boss's protection.

But she wanted so much more than that...

Then it was about time she got used to the fact she wasn't going to get it.

It seemed only moments later that Razi brought the Jeep to a halt outside a gleaming white building. Life seemed that way because it took on a frenetic pace with Razi in it, Lucy concluded as a nurse in a starched uniform escorted them to the appropriate department. It was a relief to hear they were to be seen immediately—and less of a relief when there was no offer from Razi to wait outside the room where the scan would take place. By the time she had changed into a robe he had taken a seat in front of the screen. She climbed up on the examination couch and risked a faint smile as the radiographer squeezed cold jelly on her stomach and started the hunt for their tiny child.

'Well, I can tell you you're definitely pregnant.'

Lucy gasped with shock and excitement as a hectic heartbeat broke the anxious silence. Razi remained absolutely still and utterly intent.

'And expecting a healthy baby,' the radiographer confirmed to everyone's relief.

As the tense mood in the small room relaxed, Lucy thought the amplified heartbeat was the most wonderful sound she had ever heard. It was certainly the most thrilling and the most life-changing. 'I can't believe it,' she whispered, wondering if it was possible to explode with joy. 'I can't believe my little girl is growing safe inside me—she is safe, isn't she?' she anxiously confirmed. 'There's nothing wrong, is there?' The hair was standing up on the back of her neck. The radiographer had gone very quiet. She looked at Razi for reassurance as the radiographer continued his investigations.

'Just a minute, please,' the radiographer requested, focusing all of his attention on the screen. 'Can you hear that?'

Lucy strained her ears, and only then realised she was squeezing the life out of Razi's hand. 'What is it? Tell me?'

'You're not expecting one baby,' the radiographer announced in triumph. 'You're expecting twins.'

'What?' Lucy's mind blanked with shock. Then elation, disbelief, and Wow! No way! took its place, followed swiftly by acute alarm as she raced through some terrifying financial calculations in her head.

'Are you sure?' Razi demanded tensely.

'Absolutely sure,' the radiographer assured him. 'Here…you can see for yourself.' He pointed out first one tiny little child and then the other.

Razi exclaimed in Sinnebalese. He couldn't believe it. Everything suddenly seemed more real to him. He could safely say he was ecstatic. Having heard the babies' heart-beats on the monitor, suddenly he could picture them being a family.

Razi felt a swell of pride within him and he knew then that he had to protect Lucy. He never wanted the twins or their mother to feel ashamed of who they were.

'Lucy?' Razi prompted.

She was terrified. Totally overwhelmed. All her hard-won self-belief had just taken a serious knock. She had planned to raise her baby under her own strength even if that meant doing so here in Isla de Sinnebar, but now... How could she work or support herself and her babies? Where was her security? She would be at Razi's mercy.

'Twins usually come early,' the radiographer was continuing, 'so you won't have so long to wait before you're holding them in your arms.'

She knew the man meant to be kind. She knew he was trying to reassure her, but the timescale she had been working on to support one baby had just flown out of the window.

'Aren't you pleased?' Razi demanded, touching her arm to reclaim her attention.

'I'm overwhelmed,' she said honestly.

Her mind was racing, leaving her numb from an overload of excitement, emotion, love, as well as the sense of responsibility coming her way, and most of all her fear of failure. She could be stand-up, determined and as independent-minded as she liked, but she wanted to have her independence and know that whatever happened with Razi, she could support her children. She had to try and build a stake before they were born, and then—

She found herself grabbing the arm of the radiographer and asking him to double-check.

'There is no doubt,' he said.

'Sorry,' she said, self-consciously letting go of his sleeve. 'It's just that I can't believe it.'

'Neither can I.' Razi felt a rush of jubilation speed through him. He gave her a kiss, while she, still in shock, remained stiffly unresponsive.

'I often see this reaction,' the radiographer informed them. 'Fathers are generally the ones on a high, while mothers count the cost in terms of coping and expense. But of course, in your case, that won't be a problem.'

Oh, wouldn't it? thought Lucy as the man bowed low to Razi. Why should she be any different from any other woman—especially when she had no intention of putting herself in Razi's debt? Her little family had got bigger and she couldn't support them on her own. Her fate was even more firmly in Razi's hands.

'So glad to be of service to you, Your Majesty,' the radiographer was adding. 'If there's anything else I can do for you—anything at all—please, just let me know.'

Helping Lucy down from the couch, Razi smiled the heart-stopping smile that under other circumstances would have filled her with love and confidence, but right now filled her with something much closer to apprehension.

CHAPTER SIXTEEN

OUTSIDE the hospital, Razi escorted Lucy to the Jeep, keeping a firm hold on her hand and on her shoulder.

'I'm taking you straight back to the palace,' he said, gunning the engine and roaring away. 'We'll have a brief chat there—' He held up one strong, tanned hand to silence her as his call connected. A few ecstatic phrases later he cut the line. Lucy didn't need to be fluent in Sinnebalese to get the gist. 'Aren't they shocked?' she asked as he stowed the phone.

'Shocked? Their ruling Sheikh is producing children two at a time? I should hope they're rejoicing. We're well on our way to founding a dynasty.

'Joke?' he said dryly when Lucy looked at him with concern. 'Let the world believe what it will.' He turned serious. 'The main thing for me is my children's health and happiness. Am I supposed to hide the fact that I'm delighted by the imminent arrival of twins?'

'No, of course not,' Lucy agreed faintly, except she didn't appear to be included in his plans. A new fire was burning in Razi's eyes. Since he'd discovered he was to be a father of two children his protective instincts were firing on all cylinders—and God help anyone who got in his way, including Lucy Tennant.

She couldn't have been more surprised or delighted at the immediacy with which Razi had acknowledged their babies, but on the reverse side of that coin was the fact that Razi was a king and leader of a country, and while acknowledging their children was more than she had expected it meant living life on his terms, which in turn meant yielding her freedom, especially as she was not expecting twins. And if that wasn't right for her, how could it be right for her babies?

'This is the late sheikh's palace,' Razi explained, slowing the Jeep in front of some towering golden gates. 'Until my new eco-palace is ready for occupation I'm afraid both I and my guest will have to put up with some unrestrained splendour.'

It was hard if not impossible to remain immune to Razi's upbeat mood. 'I'll do my best,' Lucy responded. But the joke was quickly over. They still had discussions ahead of them and the black-robed attendants with curving scimitars glinting at their sides didn't exactly reassure her.

'Welcome to the Palace of Bling unbridled,' Razi commented dryly as they passed beneath a golden arch. He drove on down a broad avenue that glittered as if it had been sprinkled with gold dust.

For all she knew, it had, Lucy realised, feeling another jolt to her confidence.

'Quartz crystals in the mix make the surface sparkle,' Razi explained.

There were glorious banks of flowers either side of this glittering highway, but what really claimed her attention was the massive structure rising in front of them like something out of the *Arabian Nights*. There were pink towers and white minarets standing like bookends either side of jewelled cupolas of beaten gold. If she'd been a tourist she would have been overwhelmed—she was still overwhelmed, but the last of her courage had just drained away and everything began to swim before her eyes. She felt faint and sick, knowing she didn't belong, that she could never belong and that the discussions ahead of her could only be disastrous.

'Modest, hmm?' Razi murmured dryly. 'But I call it home.

'Lucy?'

Grabbing hold of her, Razi pulled into the side. 'Drink,' he insisted passing her some water and turning the air-conditioning on full.

'Sorry, I just felt—'

'You don't have to apologise,' he insisted, still with his arm around her. 'I understand this must be overwhelming for you.' He waited until she had drunk the water and then pointed out of the window. 'I'm going to open it to the public. What do you think?'

Of walls studded with sparkling jewels—or formidable battlements decorated with pennants bearing his royal insignia? 'It's too much to take in,' she admitted, breathing a sigh of wonder.

'I'm going to use this palace to showcase our heritage. There will be a museum, as well as an art gallery—and we'll hold concerts,' he added with a grin that carved a place in her heart. 'You'll like that,' he teased. 'Karaoke?' he reminded her.

She bit back tears and smiled as if everything were wonderful, but Razi made her want so much—too much.

'Feeling better?' he confirmed. 'Ready to go on now?'

She nodded her head and sat up, tilting her chin to show her determination. She would have to get used to these bouts of weakness as well as the pangs of longing, Lucy concluded as Razi drove them the last hundred yards.

He parked up in front of a wide sweep of marble steps and then came round to help her out before the attendants even had chance to reach her door. He lifted her down and steadied her on her feet in front of him. 'Don't look so worried,' he murmured, touching her face, seemingly oblivious to the phalanx of soldiers lining up as a guard of honour. 'You've had quite a day.'

'And so have you,' she pointed out, starting to feel queasy again.

'Let me get you in the shade,' he said, ushering her forward.

Razi guided her down vaulted corridors packed with treasures. She couldn't even begin to take in such a wealth of gold and jewels and fabulous art. It would take a lifetime of visits, Lucy concluded. They came to a halt in front of an intricately decorated golden door. 'The harem,' Razi explained, holding the door for her. 'No, really,' he insisted when she looked at him in surprise. 'Though these days you're the only occupant—maybe I should do something about that…' His lips quirked. 'Triplets next time?'

There wouldn't be a next time. She understood he was only being kind. They'd discuss practicalities and then she'd go home. She didn't belong here. But at least it was cooler in the splendid golden room, though her cheeks quickly heated up when she noticed the erotic murals on the walls: beautiful women with sloe eyes and full, ruby lips, and handsome men with brooding faces. How could Razi settle for her? Not that he would. That had never been on the cards.

He led the way across a magnificent marble floor and

through an archway that led into an inner courtyard where cooling breezes and a shimmering fountain added to the relaxing ambience. He suggested she sit on a gilded bench beneath the shade of a glorious jacaranda tree frosted with frowsy pink blossom. She didn't need much persuading. The fat velvet cushions looked so inviting. But when she sat down and Razi joined her he took her hands in the type of grip a person used when they were about to tell you something you really didn't want to hear. 'Why do I think this is going to be bad?'

'At a guess? You've just had the most stunning news of your life, and your emotions are all over the place?'

But by keeping hold of her Razi wasn't helping her concerns. The fine stone fretwork blurred as she stared straight ahead, not wanting to hear anything he had to say. But she couldn't silence him.

'I want you to know everything, so you're protected from cruel gossip and innuendo. There was a marriage contract—Let me finish,' he insisted when she jerked away from him.

'It was nothing—'

'Nothing?' This was everything she'd feared. Her children would never know their father. What woman would want her husband's bastard children flaunted under her nose? At best they'd be hidden away in a remote part of the country. She couldn't stand the thought of it. She wanted to raise her children where they'd be free. 'I always knew there'd be someone,' she exclaimed, imagining a face similar to those beautiful young women she had seen depicted on the walls.

'There's no one, I promise you.' Razi took hold of her arms, bringing her in front of him. 'There's no one but you, the mother of my children.'

'But we can't always have what we want,' Lucy anticipated with eyes wide and wounded.

He didn't want to be so brutally frank with her, but while his council had applauded the forthcoming proof of his fruitfulness a foreign bride would rock the country to its very foundation—even a foreign mistress flaunted in front of the traditionalists would be a step too far. The cold truth was, he would acknowledge their children and afford them full rights and privileges, but Lucy had to go. He couldn't have Lucy and the throne so he had no option but to send her away. His life was pledged to a country—and Lucy was right. He couldn't have what he wanted any more than she could.

'You don't have to explain anything,' she said.

'Yes, I do,' he argued, touching her cheek so she had nowhere to look but in his eyes. 'And for once, you have to listen.' His duty was to defend a kingdom, to help it grow and to provide heirs, but he would do everything he could to protect Lucy from further hurt. It would take more than a few days to build her confidence in him until it could never be shaken and words wouldn't do it; he had to prove himself.

'I can't stand by and watch you with someone else, Razi. I won't.' She was growing ever more heated. 'Not when I know that no one can ever love you as I do.'

'You love me?' He was brought up short by this admission.

'You must know I love you,' she told him, frowning.

'How would I know that?'

Razi was right. She had never been brave enough to tell him that she loved him. And after everything he had confided in her she had never once told him that it could be different, that a woman could love him and that his loveless childhood was not the norm. She had been too wrapped up in the fact that a desert king with more power and wealth than she could imagine would never take up with a cook, and had never once considered that what Razi needed most was love, and that love was the one thing she could give him. She had thought him aloof, but when had she risked her feelings? She would walk through fire for him, but when had she told him that?

A cold hand gripped Lucy's throat at the thought that she had never told her parents how much she loved them either. But it was no use burying her face in her hands. She had to do something about it. She had Razi to thank for building her confidence to the point where she'd caught a glimpse of what she could be, and only herself to blame for losing her grip on that image. She was about to become a mother and that had changed her. She was a woman who was deeply in love with one man—a woman who mustn't allow the old insecurities to master her a second longer. 'Yes, I love you,' she said defiantly. 'Make what you will of that.'

He smiled inwardly at this return of the battler and he knew Lucy's words came straight from her wounded heart. He wouldn't hold her to them. He had never looked for love, let alone expected to find it. He had never guessed that Lucy felt anything more for him than passion and fascination for someone who came from a very different culture, a very different world. She had always seemed so business-like out of bed—all this talk of restaurants and shares in a business. However he felt about her was irrelevant. He'd learned to smother feelings like those years back.

He told her everything about the supposed marriage contract with his cousin and how it could never have been, and that it was a cheap trick dreamed up by Leila's father. 'He couldn't have known that as far as my own father was concerned I didn't exist. I never even met him,' he explained to an incredulous Lucy. 'My father, the ruling Sheikh of Isla de Sinnebar, never once acknowledged me during his lifetime as his son.'

'Oh, Razi—'

He shook off her tender concern. 'That's why I'm so proud to acknowledge my children—and why I'll always be there for them—' He stopped, seeing the fear in her eyes. This was about reassuring Lucy, not about him. 'As my father never mentioned me, why would he arrange a marriage for me? I knew at once that the document Leila's father presented was a forgery, but I had it scrutinised by experts, just to be sure. And now it's all been put to bed.'

'With a large pay-off?' she interrupted, still fearing the worst.

He could see where this was going. 'Lucy, this is nothing like your situation.'

She pulled her hands out of his grasp.

'Things are going to be very different for you,' he stressed. 'I only wish there was time now for me to lay out all the plans I've made for you.'

'You've made plans for me?' she said softly.

He glanced around. 'Can't you see one of your wonderful restaurants here in this courtyard once I open this palace to the public? A café in the courtyard—and perhaps another restaurant for gourmet eating in the gardens?'

He was all fired up with his plans for Lucy's future, but at the back of his mind was the knowledge that he must shower and change into formal attire before the council meeting...

The more he thought about the meeting, the more he

thought about what could be if life were shunted onto a different track. And he could do that. He could do anything he wanted to as long as it embraced his vow to Isla de Sinnebar...

Now a plan was forming in his mind. He felt quite cool and certain as he mulled it over. This was right. It was hard to understand why he hadn't seen it before. 'I have a meeting,' he explained to Lucy, 'and I can't be late.' He was becoming more eager to take the action that would irrevocably change his life.

'Razi, wait,' Lucy said, picking up on his sense of urgency.

Taking hold of her hands, he pressed his lips to the palm of each of them in turn, and then, cursing softly in Sinnebalese, he shook his head regretfully. 'There's never enough time.'

'No, I can see that,' she said quietly.

'I'll have a maid show you to your room. A bath has been run for you.' He was already striding away. 'Food and juices are waiting for you along with your luggage.' He turned at the door to shoot her a grin. 'You might want to change your clothes and relax while I'm gone. Take a swim. Ask for a guided tour of the palace. Do anything you want to do.' He felt exhilarated and sure, though acutely conscious of the clock ticking as he spread his arms wide to bow and back away. 'Take care, mother of my children. Relax in the knowledge that from this moment on your life is transformed. Oh, and I'll be back before you know it,' he added with a wicked grin.

This time when Razi's lips tugged in the familiar heart-stopping smile, Lucy couldn't return his smile. Her life had been transformed, both by pregnancy and today by the knowledge that two small lives depended on her. She was a woman of purpose now, not a mistress of idleness who needed her days filling with aimless meandering. Was Razi's offer of creating a restaurant here at the palace a sop to keep her happy? She didn't know what to believe any more.

As she watched him stride away it was easy to see that Razi's life was full of purpose, but if he imagined she was going to live to his prescription—wait until he could find time for her, as his mother had waited—or, worse still, that he would be hard-pressed to find space in his packed diary for their children, he had underestimated the woman he had helped to grow in confidence. She loved him and to Lucy love meant working together to build a future. If she could never be his wife, she could at least put her skills at the service of his country. Razi had mentioned an eco-palace in construction, hadn't he? And a palace would have kitchens…

As she picked up the internal phone to call for transport Lucy realised she was not going to go back to England and consult lawyers, she was going to stay here in Isla de Sinnebar. She would live in some remote part where she could cause Razi no embarrassment, but she would keep her children with her and she would work for the good of Razi's people. And if that meant being a pioneer, setting a new trend, fine, that was what she'd do. She'd work discreetly so as not to offend anyone, but she'd do it, Lucy concluded, jutting out her chin.

CHAPTER SEVENTEEN

HE NEVER failed to feel a sense of history when he entered the golden chamber—the vaulted roofs, the jewelled panelled walls, the silent air of majesty. As all the men currently seated around the council table rose to greet him he was conscious of their wise faces turned to him and the trust in so many pairs of eyes. He stood for a moment, feeling the weight of destiny in his hands. He indicated that everyone should sit down, while he remained standing at the head of the table. He was prepared to sacrifice everything for Lucy. He had known this from the moment he had realised that a life of lies and self-deception wasn't for him.

He greeted his brother sheikhs and then repeated the wonderful news about his twins. Then to absolute silence he explained his proposal before calling on his council to vote on his decision to cede the Phoenix throne in favour of working alongside the woman he loved as a common man for the good of Isla de Sinnebar and his people. He finished by saying, 'I want you all to know that the decision I have made has been mine and mine alone. This was a thing I had to judge entirely for myself.'

Now he could only wait for their verdict.

He didn't have to wait long. The oldest and most trusted

advisor spoke for the rest. They supported him whole-heartedly. They believed in his vision of the future. If that vision included a foreign bride, they supported him in that too. He would keep the throne and their trust. Then they raised their fists and hailed him until they were hoarse as their undisputed leader.

'Stop the cavalcade!'

He sprang out of the lead limousine before it had drawn to a halt. Full of concern for Lucy's safety, he thanked destiny for urging him to see his new eco-palace in construction before he went on to his next meeting. He was eager to see Lucy too and his plan had been to conclude his business as swiftly as he could before driving straight back to her with his news. It had never occurred to him that he would arrive at the site of his new palace to find a pregnant woman in jeans, sneakers and a high-visibility jacket with a hard hat on her head and clipboard in her hand, conferring with Asif, his site manager.

His first action was to order his security staff to stay with the cavalcade. His second was to stride over to Lucy.

'What do you think you're doing?'

'Working,' she said, giving him a look he hadn't seen before.

For once he rued the fact that official limousines had blacked-out windows, but he didn't need to see inside the vehicles to know that everyone in the official party would be riveted by this unexpected distraction. 'Do you have to do this? Can't you see how dangerous it is?'

'Dangerous?' She frowned. 'I'm in no danger. Are you sure it isn't the idea of a woman working that's getting to you, Razi?'

Asif faded into the background with a respectful bow.

'You're pregnant.'

'Yes—not ill.'

'You're putting yourself in danger on a building site.'

'Asif was with me and now you're here. I'm appropriately dressed and I won't take any risks.'

'You don't have to work.'

The scorching look she gave him said Lucy would never subscribe to the world's view of how a wealthy man's lover should behave, but would plough her own furrow. Did he like that? Could his vaunted ego take it?

He had the opportunity to start a new page in the history of Isla de Sinnebar, one where opportunity was open to all, and there were no gender divides where jobs were concerned. He could use his vast wealth to change lives and Lucy wanted to be part of that—he wanted her to be part of it. As she stared up at him and firmed her dainty jaw he wondered if he'd left it too late to convince her he wasn't the tyrant she thought him—too late to explain that she didn't have to go to extremes to escape his mother's fate?

'I thought you were different, but you're such a dinosaur, Razi.'

'Am I?' he said dryly as she turned away.

'Women shouldn't do men's work?' She tipped her chin as she stopped to confront him. 'You can probably set it down in law now you've got the country at your command.'

'I can definitely send you back to the palace.'

'Where I can write my report? Good,' she said, refusing to be dismayed. 'I'll have it ready for you on your return.'

She was standing in the harem by the console table she had turned into a desk when Razi entered. She didn't need to turn around to know he was there or that he was still dressed in robes. She could hear the swish of the fabric as he walked towards her and inhale its scented folds. She remained standing, with her back turned to him, staring out across the shaded courtyard dreaming of all the things she would like to change in Isla de Sinnebar, given the opportunity. Razi, for one.

'Lucy…'

The swish of his robes, the click of the prayer beads at his waist, the fine, clean scent…

She turned, her heart juddering at the sight of him. She would never, no matter how long she knew him, become accustomed to the sight of Razi. It was more than his astonishing good looks. When he was in western clothes Razi carried the scent of soap and toothpaste and warm clean man, but the robes of state added the spices of the East and the unmistakeable scent of power. He was a formidable sight, an untouchable sight, this man she loved.

'What do you have to say?' he said quietly.

She intended to be calm and rational, but in the event it all burst out of her. 'I want you to be proud of me—I want my children to have a mother who leads from the front—'

'And you have to work on a building site to do that?'

'Whatever it takes! I realise it wouldn't be right for everyone, but I want to work. I want to earn my keep. I don't want to be your mistress-in-waiting.' Her voice broke. She had every intention of making a stand, or reminding him of his mother's plight, but pregnancy had made her so emotional and all she could think about was Razi's mother waiting in this same room, looking out at the same view as she waited for a ruling Sheikh around whom Helena's world had revolved. 'I want to make a difference.'

'You can do that without working on a building site!'

'Don't roar at me.' She hugged herself. 'I'm pregnant.'

Now they both almost laughed.

'I didn't mean to embarrass you, Razi. I just thought if I could talk to Asif and the architects on site before they put the kitchen walls in place I could come up with a really good working plan…' Her voice tailed away. Razi's expression was inscrutable.

Seconds ticked by tensely and then his gaze flicked over the papers she had laid out on the table. 'And are these your notes?'

'Yes…'

He walked past her and stood, staring down, and then he picked up her clipboard. Having scanned her bullet-pointed notes and the scheme she had sketched out, he admitted, 'This is good.'

She had to tamp down the excitement inside her. If she was going to stay here she had to prove herself effective. 'I thought if the kitchens could cater for the largest event— or just a family meal—and you have sections that can be brought into play, or shut off—'

'Yes, I see,' Razi said thoughtfully. 'We'll sit down with the architects tomorrow and discuss this in detail.'

'We will?'

'Unless you don't want to be part of the discussions?'

'Of course I do.' Her head was immediately full of more ideas.

'Well? What did you think of the site I chose for the eco-palace?' he probed, acting nonchalant as if it didn't matter hugely to him.

Did love at first sight work with a building site? It just had, Lucy concluded. Yes, there were cranes and diggers and portable buildings and containers, not to mention squads of men in hard hats and high-visibility vests swarming over the scaffolding, but the site itself, framed by mountains and bordered by a sparkling river of the same ice-cold water she had bathed in back at the oasis, was nothing short of fabulous. She'd stood in silence, breathing the warm, spicy air, knowing it was where she wanted to be.

And could never be, because one day Razi must take a wife.

'Well?' he demanded. 'First impressions?'

She refocused on Razi's project—his palace, his life—and, with the utmost reluctance, her reality. 'You're very lucky.' She remembered the wise old site manager, Asif, wearing a bright yellow hard hat over his headdress waving to her as she was driven away. She'd waved back, wondering if she'd ever see the building site again. 'It's absolutely beautiful,' she confessed wistfully, 'and the possibilities are endless.' Unfortunately, the possibilities open to her were not.

'You know I'd never keep you here against your will?' Razi demanded softly, running a fingertip down her cheek. 'With your talents you have so much to offer the world.'

He pulled away to look around. 'Seeing you here in this place that was almost a prison for my mother—' His mouth clamped shut and she knew what he was feeling. 'The bird in the gilded cage.' He laughed, but there was no humour in his voice. 'There'll never be another,' he vowed, almost as if speaking to himself.

He ran his fingers across her makeshift desk, which Lucy suddenly realised was almost certainly made of solid gold. 'All this excess brought my mother nothing but misery.' Razi's angry gesture at something he couldn't change ripped her heart out. 'All this extravagant glitter is tainted with sadness, which is why I could never live here.' His eyes were fierce with the need for her to understand. 'I just hope that when I turn it over to the public—'

'It will be a wonderful and happy place,' Lucy exclaimed, unable to keep quiet a moment longer. 'I can see it now—facilities for culture and education…and for fun, Razi.' She smiled with encouragement as ideas for the palace bombarded her. She couldn't have been happier that Razi intended preserving the old palace so people could see how previous generations had lived. Whatever the history behind it, the workmanship was astonishing— the mosaics, the gold work, the mirrors, framed with carved gilt figures and tumbling ribbons so finely worked. 'I promise you,' she exclaimed with passion, 'this is going to be a great attraction. I can see it now. This old palace will come alive for all sorts of people and will become a talking point in the worldwide tourist industry. I doubt anyone could come up with a better competitive differential, if they tried.'

'A competitive differential?' Razi interrupted.

Was that humour on his face?

'Are you intending to become a businesswoman now?'

'I do have dreams,' she admitted.

'Some people—and I am one of them—would call that vision. They would go on to say that certain people are blessed with the determination to make that vision concrete, and that those people make a real difference in the world.' Picking up the scheme she'd drawn, he added, 'It seems to me like you've taken the first step towards doing that with this plan of yours.'

She reached out to take the drawing from him, but he wouldn't let it go. 'First a cake tin,' he murmured dryly, his green eyes so warm with humour she thought her heart would burst with happiness, 'and now a kitchen design.' He smiled the slow, sexy smile she realised in that moment she had been desperately starved of.

'Perhaps it's time to inject a little romance into this relationship?' he suggested darkly.

'I thought we were going to sit down and talk?'

'I do have something to tell you,' he admitted, 'but it can wait.'

Somehow, Razi's hand had enclosed hers and the drawings he'd been holding were back on the table.

Am I dreaming? Lucy wondered as he drew her into his arms. Should she pinch herself? 'Razi…?' Her eyes searched his. 'Where do we go from here?'

'Speaking for myself,' he said dryly, 'I'm finding it hard to get past the sight of you in your hard hat—though I'd make a few changes,' he admitted, his expression growing serious.

'You would?' she said anxiously.

'Yes…' He touched her arms lightly, which was enough for her body to respond with indecent eagerness to nothing more than the brush of his fingertips. 'I'd cancel the jeans, and dress you in a pair of very short shorts. The heavy boots could stay—they set off your fabulous legs.' He shrugged. 'The clipboard and pen could stay too—though I'd add a pair of really heavy specs so you look incredibly stern and enormously severe.'

'Razi…I don't know what to say.'

'There's no need to talk at all—unless you have some suggestions of your own to make?'

CHAPTER EIGHTEEN

'SUGGESTIONS of my own?' Thoroughly caught up in Razi's mood, Lucy forced a frown as she pretended to think about it. 'I'm happy to leave it all up to you—but just remember one thing.'

'Which is?' Heat radiated from him as he eased onto one hip.

'You're mine. And I'll never let you go.'

His face creased in the familiar grin. 'It's about time we agreed on something.'

Passion scorched through her like a lava stream as he dragged her into his arms. 'Well?' she managed to fire back as he stared down at her. 'I need you.' She writhed against him with frustration to prove how much.

'You think I don't know that?' His laugh was low and husky and amused.

It was Mac's voice—Razi's voice—the voice she loved. It was the tone of voice she had missed and adored—the voice of the man she loved.

And the wall—with its lurid depictions of lovemaking in every form—was the best friend she'd ever had, Lucy registered wildly, consumed by savage heat as Razi stripped her naked before proving how fast a desert king could lose his robe.

He had her at the first thrust. He was everything she wanted, and if there was a way for them all to be together, she felt that now they stood a chance of finding it.

Throwing back her head, she urged him on, while Razi loved her with an insatiable hunger that matched her own. He was her man, her mate. She loved him and she would fight for him with everything she'd got. She wailed convulsively as the first climax hit her, but instead of releasing him she dug her fingers into his shoulders and wrapped her legs even more tightly around his waist, daring him to let her go.

'Let you go?' Razi's lips tugged with amusement as he briefly paused. 'I would sooner join a monastery than consider life without you.'

'Don't you dare lie to me,' she warned him, sinking her teeth into his shoulder, before gasping with surprise and pleasure when he pounded into her again. 'And don't you dare stop until I tell you to stop,' she added fiercely, shrieking with pleasure as he bounced her hips against the wall.

But when she felt the tidal wave of pleasure was close it was time to bring some plans of her own into play. 'Now slowly,' she ordered him, relishing every deep, lingering thrust. And when his guard was down in those few last moments before she too would lose control, she took him to the hilt, and, using her muscles, worked him in a way she knew he loved until it was Razi who broke first and she who soothed him down in triumph. 'You're mine,' she told him fiercely as his heartbeat steadied. 'Mine—and I won't share you with anyone.'

'Share me?' Razi demanded with amusement as he lowered her carefully to the ground. 'Do you really think there would be anything left by the time you've finished with me?'

Glancing down, she hummed. 'I don't know, there seems plenty…'

'Only because I'm with you.' Dipping his head, he stared into her eyes. 'That's why I don't need or want anyone else.'

'What about when you're married?'

'I'll want you twice as much.'

She looked at him aghast when he laughed. 'But your wife,' she choked out as all the old doubts reared up to taunt her. She was what Razi wanted in bed, but she had always known that when it came to choosing a bride it would have to be a diplomatic match for the good of the kingdom. What would that mean for her babies? She could be as determined as she liked, but she could never bear the pain of seeing another woman at Razi's side.

'I don't want anyone else,' Razi reassured her, staring into her eyes. 'Why should I?'

She wasn't listening. 'I thought I could handle anything to be with you, but I can't take my happiness at someone else's expense—I could never do any of the things required of a mistress.'

'Will you calm down?' Razi demanded gently. 'You're upsetting the babies.'

'You fight dirty,' Lucy protested, only quietening when Razi wrapped his arms around her.

'I never said I'd play fair.'

'So what happens next?'

'What happens next will be set down in law,' he soothed her. 'I will make you my wife so I can keep you working. Oh, yes, I'll make you work,' he said when she looked at him.

'Wait, wait, wait—wind back a bit. Did you say wife?'

'There's plenty to stretch your talents here in Isla de Sinnebar—and I wouldn't dream of wasting such a valuable resource.'

'Razi,' she cut in. 'Are you teasing me or are you serious?'

'Do I mean you're going to work? Absolutely. Do I mean you're going to be my wife? Yes—if you'll have me?'

'Oh, yes, yes, yes—I think I can safely assure you I'd be happy to accept both positions. But what about your people? They would never accept me—'

'They already have.'

'What? How can they? Please stop teasing me and explain.'

'There's no need to bore you with the detail—one day, maybe,' he said softly. 'Let's just say they truly welcome you as their Queen. Oh, and did I mention how hard you'll be working?'

'You did say something,' she agreed dryly, smiling into his eyes.

'Along with being my first, my best, my only wife, and the only woman I will ever love for the rest of my life, you're going to be in charge of all the royal catering facilities as well as the mother of two children. That should satisfy all your feminist inclinations and keep you out of mischief for the foreseeable future.'

She looked at him and for a long moment neither of them spoke. 'So you really are serious?' she said at last.

'Of course I'm serious.'

'We're to be married…'

'How could I let you go when I've watched you sleeping in my arms, when I've seen the dawn dust your skin with gold and watched your eyes light with love and happiness—'

'And you're a romantic?'

'Of course.' Razi's face creased in the familiar smile. 'How's this? Even your shadow throws light.'

'Hmm—not bad.'

'Or this—I won't let you go.'

Did he mean it?

'But what about Isla de Sinnebar?' she said, turning serious.

'All the more reason for me to do what is right. And this is right, Lucy.'

Razi spoke with such confidence that when he started whispering to her in his own language in a way that soothed and convinced and seduced all at the same time it took all she'd got to root out her last doubt. 'So I won't be locked away in some love nest?'

'That's a colourful picture,' he murmured, backing her slowly across the room. 'Locking you in the kitchen, I could understand...'

They shared a look that told Lucy the mistakes of the past would never be repeated, and then they embraced, fiercely and passionately until they sank to the floor where they stood. This time Razi's lovemaking was slow and tender. He used all his skill to draw out her pleasure, and all the while he told her how much he loved her. By the time he released her they had moved far beyond hurt and confusion to a new ease and confidence that bound them together in a way that words never could.

They showered together—which took quite a lot of time. Fortunately, they dressed much faster, and then Razi drove Lucy back to the building site that would soon be his new palace, and, incredibly, their family home. Knowing they would live together in such a beautiful place was almost more than Lucy could take in and she made Razi tell her it was so over and over again.

It was as if she was seeing the half-finished building through completely new eyes, she realised when he finally convinced her. Had she noticed how seamlessly the sandstone structure blended into the desert landscape? Or how the purple mountains surrounding it provided a majestic frame? The colours seemed more vivid than ever—the golden sand and turquoise ocean, the green of the parkland being carefully cultivated in front of the lagoon where one day soon their children would play. This truly was the place where reality and fantasy met.

'You have no idea how much I love you—or how amazing you look,' Razi observed with a grin as they linked fingers.

They had both chosen to wear traditional robes for this visit to their new home. Razi's robe was heavy blue silk with a matching flowing headpiece and a gold *agal*, while Lucy's robe was softer sky-blue chiffon trimmed with silver embroidery, and she had to admit she felt a lot cooler than she would have done in western clothes.

'Are you happy?' Razi demanded, bringing her round to face him.

'I can't begin to tell you.'

'Then I'll have to find a way,' he said as he drew her into the shadows where her pale skin wouldn't burn.

As he caressed her face she caught hold of his hand and brought it to her cheek. 'I love you,' she whispered, still finding it incredible that she could say that, and that this strong, dark prince of the desert had told her that he loved her in return.

'You're so much more than I deserve,' he said, and when

she looked at him in surprise he shook his head. 'Why can't you believe how special you are?'

'Because I'm nothing special?' Lucy announced in her usual blunt way.

'Nothing special?' Throwing back his head, Razi laughed. 'I think you're looking for compliments,' he accused as the desert wind whipped his hair into a tangle.

Before she had chance to deny this, he added, 'You're brave and determined and strong—not to mention capable and talented.'

'Go on—I can't get enough of this now. Though you are starting to make me sound a like a trick pony.'

Razi narrowed his eyes. 'I was about to add—and sexier than any woman has any right to be.'

'That's much better,' Lucy approved, sharing Razi's smile.

'I love you, Lucy Tennant,' he stated frankly. 'And I want to share my life with you.'

'No ifs, buts, or maybes?' she said wryly.

'No doubts ever. And if I have to spend the rest of my life convincing you, then I'll sign up now. You're the only woman I want. You're the only mother I could ever want for my children.'

'Why?'

'Because I know you'll fight with everything you've got for them, and for me, and for all the people of the Isla de Sinnebar when they call you their Queen.'

'Their Queen?' Lucy echoed incredulously.

'Why so surprised?' Razi demanded with a nonchalant shrug. 'Haven't you realised yet that I'll stop at nothing to keep a good chef?'

EPILOGUE

THE women came for her at dawn. Lucy had spent the night in the tented city amongst her people, guarded by the royal security troops. But she longed for Razi. She longed for the last of the barriers keeping them apart to be removed. And, yes, she longed to step beyond the silken veil. The women Razi had sent to prepare her for their Sheikh would help her do that. Clothed in colourful robes like so many jewelled butterflies, they clustered round her, kohl-lined eyes smiling with excitement.

Slipping off her sandals, Lucy padded wide-eyed into the bridal tent, her own private sanctuary of luxury and warmth. Light streamed from a thousand tiny brass lanterns, and there was incense burning. Soft carpets tickled her feet and plump cushions in shades of soft pink and burnished gold were arranged all around the perimeter of the uniquely feminine pavilion. There was fruit and jugs of juice, and honeyed pastries piled in tempting mountains on low pierced brass tables, but Lucy had only one thought in her mind, and that was Razi. Only he could satisfy the hunger she felt now.

They bathed her in warm, scented water, before drying her on the softest of towels. Every hair on her body, other than her waist-length, honey-coloured tresses, her eye-brows and eyelashes, was then painstakingly removed—with the emphasis on pain, Lucy registered, biting down hard on her bottom lip as she told herself it would all be worth it if she could just keep in mind the rewards that would definitely follow.

After this they brushed her body until it tingled, before massaging her with fragrant oils that added to her sensi-tivity. Then she stood with all the confidence in her naked body Razi had given her and raised her hands as they slipped a cobweb-fine shift over her head. Next they seated her on cushions where she had her hands and feet deco-rated with intricate swirls and dots of henna, and when that was done her clean, scented hair was first polished with silk and then braided loosely.

Only then did they bring out the wedding robe she had chosen. In the palest shade of pink silk chiffon, it twinkled with diamonds and platinum hand-embroidery. There were jewelled slippers for her feet, and she would carry in her hands the good wishes of her people represented by semi-precious stones and gold coins painstakingly threaded onto a great ribbon of glittering light that would dazzle as she walked. This traditional royal Sinnebalese wedding scarf would be wound around her hands and Razi's during the ceremony that followed, binding them together for all eternity.

'There's just one more thing,' one of the women told her as they arranged Lucy's veil. 'A gift from the Sheikh,' she said, laying the golden casket at Lucy's feet.

'We need what's inside to secure your veil,' the same woman confided as Lucy trailed her fingertips across the intricately worked golden box. Trust Razi to put a packet of kirby grips in a gold box the size of this one, she was thinking before she opened the lid.

She gasped in shock. It appeared Razi's economies had bypassed his wedding gift to her. Nestled snugly on a night blue velvet ground, a fabulous chain of pink and white diamonds flamed and glittered with all the colours of the rainbow. She touched them reverently and then pulled her hand away. 'I can't—I mean, I don't—'

'Don't worry, Sheikha,' one of the hand-maidens told her. 'We'll arrange them for you…'

'I'm going to wear them?' She sat stock-still as they draped her in diamonds that felt surprisingly cool and soothing against her brow. The large central diadem, which was the size of the pigeon's egg, counterbalanced the weight of the rest so it held her veil in place. Diamonds were far more effective than kirby grips, Lucy conceded dryly as one of the women held up a mirror so she could see her reflection.

'Now do you see why I love you?'

At the sound of Razi's voice, all the women got up in a rustle of skirts, bowing low to their Sheikh as they backed their way out of the bridal pavilion.

'Should you be here?' Lucy demanded, slanting kohl-enhanced eyes to drink him in.

'I do as I please.' He said this with all the old humour. 'And I'm pleased to see you have taken to your new role as if to the manner born.'

'Like you?' Lucy suggested wryly. They shared a look that said neither of them had been born to this, but they were both ready to devote themselves to the country and to their family, and to each other.

'The old days are over,' Razi said, bringing Lucy to her feet in front of him. 'We will walk to our wedding as equals.'

'Some of the old ways are worth preserving…'

'Do I take it that means you enjoyed your preparations?'

'Being prepared for the Sheikh?' She shrugged ruefully. 'Yes, I liked most of it—though some of it was painful.'

'They hurt you?'

'I shall expect a suitable reward.'

'Then I must ensure that you get it.'

She exclaimed with delight as Razi teased her with his lips and with his teeth and with his tongue. 'I'll hold you to that.'

'Just hold me,' he said, inhaling deeply as he dropped kisses on her neck. 'Amber, jasmine and lemon grass.'

'The scent you designed for me.'

'And which will be all you wear tonight, and for every night from now on.'

She shivered with delicious anticipation as Razi took her hand in his.

She barely noticed anything for the next hour, other than the man at her side in his warrior robes of unrelieved black. Razi was a magnificent sight. Beyond the heavy gold *agal* holding his headdress in place and the fearsome Khanjar at his waist, he needed no decoration, and when he placed the diamond band onto her wedding finger and pledged his love, she knew that sometimes fairy tales did come true. He was her warrior king, her dark prince of the desert, and she loved him more than life itself.

What would her rowdy brothers make of little Lucy now? she wondered as the marriage ceremony ended in fierce shouts of joy from the throats of thousands of tribesmen seated on horseback. Her whole family had fallen silent for the first time that she could remember at the news that she was expecting twins, and then the noisiest discussion she could remember had broken out on the subject of whether some men had unusual advantages in the fertility stakes—one discussion she really hadn't wanted to get into.

As soon as the marriage ceremony on the beach beneath the flower-strewn canopy was over Razi's first duty was to lead her towards the Phoenix throne and present her to his brother, Ra'id, who had been seated in Razi's place for this one day to show him honour. Lucy shivered, remembering Ra'id was known as The Sword of Vengeance. Her first sight of him had left a fearsome impression of a dark force of nature lit by molten rays of sunlight shimmering around the golden throne that seemed to frame him in a ring of fire. She tensed as Ra'id stood and his shadow fell across her. He was a stern, darkly handsome man, who, having dipped his head to acknowledge her, embraced his brother warmly.

'What do you think of Ra'id?' Razi murmured as they walked on.

She was still shaken by the meeting, but she opted for the truth. 'He looks lonely.'

'Lonely?' Razi demanded incredulously. 'The man known as The Sword of Vengeance, lonely?' He shook his head as if she had a lot to learn. 'My brother, Ra'id, is the most powerful man in the Middle East.'

'And even powerful men need someone to love and need to be loved in return,' she insisted.

Razi smiled at her. 'Then I can only hope my brother is as lucky in love as I have been.'

'As we have been...'

Razi squeezed her hand. 'As we have been,' he repeated softly.

Her family was struck dumb again and it was a shock to see her mother crying. 'I love you,' Lucy said, touching her mother's arm.

They shared a glance, and then to her surprise her mother grasped her hand and brought it to her lips. 'I love you too,' she said, almost with desperation in her voice.

'We'll see them later,' Razi told Lucy to reassure her as the bridal procession moved on. 'The wedding celebrations continue for a week.'

'A week?'

The concern in her voice made him smile. 'Sadly, we have a prior engagement that will keep us away for the first half day.'

'Oh, no.' Then seeing the stallion waiting for them, caparisoned in gold and traditionally woven fabrics, she understood. Springing up, Razi lifted her in front of him and in a flurry of hooves they galloped away.

'Another tradition,' he assured her, holding her close as he acknowledged the cheers of the tribesmen as they rode the length of the seashore. But instead of turning back to return to the wedding party, he rode on towards a beach over the dunes and out of sight.

'Razi, we can't do this,' Lucy exclaimed, glancing over her shoulder.

'If you think I'm going to waste a single moment when I know you've been prepared for the Sheikh…' Reining in the stallion, he sprang to the ground and, reaching up, brought her down beside him.

They fell into each other's arms, kissing tenderly, deeply, passionately, rejoicing in this, their first kiss as husband and wife. Then, ever the pragmatist, Razi eased

Lucy's wedding robe from her shoulders and let it drop to the ground.

'Wow, that was easy,' Lucy remarked. 'Let's hope this form of traditional dress never goes out of fashion.'

Razi's face creased in a smile as he viewed the scattered silk. 'No buttons—no zips?' He shrugged. 'Who's going to better that design?'

'I agree.' Raising her arms, Lucy laced her fingers through Razi's thick, strong hair. 'So? What do you think, Your Majesty?'

'What do I think?' He shrugged off his robe and tossed his headdress aside, before kneeling at her feet. 'I think there are quite a few old customs worth preserving.'

She moaned with pleasure as he tasted her and his stubble scraped her newly naked skin. 'Another tradition?' she managed breathlessly.

'It will be,' he assured her.

Some considerable time later, when they had emerged from the bath-warm ocean, Razi found something in the pocket of his robe.

'What is it?' Lucy said as he first teased her and then slowly unfurled his hand. She gasped when she saw the dainty replica of her wedding ring studded in diamonds.

'I had it made so you can add it to the tiny slipper you wear to remind you that your prince has come.'

'Again?'

Razi laughed as he added the ring to the fine chain around her neck, and when they'd stopped laughing Lucy turned serious. 'Razi, what can I possibly give you to compare with all your fabulous wedding gifts to me?'

'Two babies?' Razi suggested dryly. 'Quite a bonus, I'd say—when all I've ever wanted is your love.' He grinned.

'But I'm sure I'll think of something else, given enough time. And as we have all the time in the world ahead of us…'

'Amen to that,' Lucy said softly as Razi kissed her.

HARLEQUIN *Presents*

Coming Next Month

in **Harlequin Presents®**. Available July 27, 2010.

#2933 THE ITALIAN DUKE'S VIRGIN MISTRESS
Penny Jordan

#2934 MIA AND THE POWERFUL GREEK
Michelle Reid
The Balfour Brides

#2935 THE GREEK'S PREGNANT LOVER
Lucy Monroe
Traditional Greek Husbands

#2936 AN HEIR FOR THE MILLIONAIRE
Carole Mortimer and Julia James
2 in 1

#2937 COUNT TOUSSAINT'S BABY
Kate Hewitt

#2938 MASTER OF THE DESERT
Susan Stephens

Coming Next Month

in **Harlequin Presents® EXTRA**. Available August 10, 2010.

#113 SWEET SURRENDER WITH THE MILLIONAIRE
Helen Brooks
British Bachelors

#114 SECRETARY BY DAY, MISTRESS BY NIGHT
Maggie Cox
British Bachelors

#115 TO LOVE, HONOR AND DISOBEY
Natalie Anderson
Conveniently Wedded...& Bedded

#116 WEDDING NIGHT WITH A STRANGER
Anna Cleary
Conveniently Wedded...& Bedded

LARGER-PRINT BOOKS!

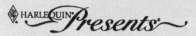

HARLEQUIN *Presents*~

PASSION GUARANTEED SEDUCTION

GET 2 FREE LARGER-PRINT NOVELS PLUS 2 FREE GIFTS!

YES! Please send me 2 FREE LARGER-PRINT Harlequin Presents® novels and my 2 FREE gifts (gifts are worth about $10). After receiving them, if I don't wish to receive any more books, I can return the shipping statement marked "cancel". If I don't cancel, I will receive 6 brand-new novels every month and be billed just $4.55 per book in the U.S. or $5.24 per book in Canada. That's a saving of at least 13% off the cover price! It's quite a bargain! Shipping and handling is just 50¢ per book.* I understand that accepting the 2 free books and gifts places me under no obligation to buy anything. I can always return a shipment and cancel at any time. Even if I never buy another book, the two free books and gifts are mine to keep forever.

176/376 HDN E5NG

Name	(PLEASE PRINT)

Address	Apt. #

City	State/Prov.	Zip/Postal Code

Signature (if under 18, a parent or guardian must sign)

Mail to the **Harlequin Reader Service:**
IN U.S.A.: P.O. Box 1867, Buffalo, NY 14240-1867
IN CANADA: P.O. Box 609, Fort Erie, Ontario L2A 5X3

Not valid for current subscribers to Harlequin Presents Larger-Print books.

Are you a subscriber to Harlequin Presents books and want to receive the larger-print edition?
Call 1-800-873-8635 today!

* Terms and prices subject to change without notice. Prices do not include applicable taxes. Sales tax applicable in N.Y. Canadian residents will be charged applicable provincial taxes and GST. Offer not valid in Quebec. This offer is limited to one order per household. All orders subject to approval. Credit or debit balances in a customer's account(s) may be offset by any other outstanding balance owed by or to the customer. Please allow 4 to 6 weeks for delivery. Offer available while quantities last.

Your Privacy: Harlequin Books is committed to protecting your privacy. Our Privacy Policy is available online at www.eHarlequin.com or upon request from the Reader Service. From time to time we make our lists of customers available to reputable third parties who may have a product or service of interest to you. If you would prefer we not share your name and address, please check here. ☐

Help us get it right—We strive for accurate, respectful and relevant communications. To clarify or modify your communication preferences, visit us at www.ReaderService.com/consumerschoice.

HPLP10R

HARLEQUIN®

A *Romance*

FOR EVERY MOOD™

Spotlight on
— Heart & Home —

Heartwarming romances
where love can happen
right when you least expect it.

See the next page to enjoy a sneak peek
from Harlequin® American Romance®,
a Heart and Home series.

CATHHHAR10

Five hunky Texas single fathers—five stories from Cathy Gillen Thacker's LONE STAR DADS miniseries. Here's an excerpt from the latest, THE MOMMY PROPOSAL from Harlequin American Romance.

"I hear you work miracles," Nate Hutchinson drawled. Brooke Mitchell had just stepped into his lavishly appointed office in downtown Fort Worth, Texas.

"Sometimes, I do." Brooke smiled and took the sexy financier's hand in hers, shook it briefly.

"Good." Nate looked her straight in the eye. "Because I'm in need of a home makeover—fast. The son of an old friend is coming to live with me."

She was still tingling from the feel of his warm palm. "Temporarily or permanently?"

"If all goes according to plan, I'll adopt Landry by summer's end."

Brooke had heard the founder of Nate Hutchinson Financial Services was eligible, wealthy and generous to a fault. She hadn't known he was in the market for a family, but she supposed she shouldn't be surprised. But Brooke had figured a man as successful and handsome as Nate would want one the old-fashioned way. *Not that this was any of her business...*

"So what's the child like?" she asked crisply, trying not to think how the marine-blue of Nate's dress shirt deepened the hue of his eyes.

"I don't know." Nate took a seat behind his massive antique mahogany desk. He relaxed against the smooth leather of the chair. "I've never met him."

"Yet you've invited this kid to live with you permanently?"

"It's complicated. But I'm sure it's going to be fine."

Obviously Nate Hutchinson knew as little about teenage

boys as he did about decorating. But that wasn't her problem. Finding a way to do the assignment without getting the least bit emotionally involved was.

Find out how a young boy brings Nate and Brooke together in THE MOMMY PROPOSAL, coming August 2010 from Harlequin American Romance.

Copyright © 2010 by Cathy Gillen Thacker

The Balfour Brides

A powerful dynasty,
eight daughters in disgrace…

Absolute scandal has rocked the core of the infamous
Balfour family. The glittering, gorgeous daughters are in
disgrace…. Banished from the Balfour mansion, they're
sent to the boldest, most magnificent men
to be wedded, bedded…and tamed!

And so begins a scandalous saga of dazzling glamour
and passionate surrender.

Beginning August 2010

MIA AND THE POWERFUL GREEK—*Michelle Reid*
KAT AND THE DAREDEVIL SPANIARD—*Sharon Kendrick*
EMILY AND THE NOTORIOUS PRINCE—*India Grey*
SOPHIE AND THE SCORCHING SICILIAN—*Kim Lawrence*
ZOE AND THE TORMENTED TYCOON—*Kate Hewitt*
ANNIE AND THE RED-HOT ITALIAN—*Carol Mortimer*
BELLA AND THE MERCILESS SHEIKH—*Sarah Morgan*
OLIVIA AND THE BILLIONAIRE CATTLE KING—*Margaret Way*

8 volumes to collect and treasure!

---

www.eHarlequin.com

HP12934